THE COLLECTION

A REVERSE HAREM ROMANCE

MIKA LANE

HEADLANDS PUBLISHING

BE THE FIRST TO KNOW...

Want more heat, heart,
and bad boys who know what they're doing?
Join my list and I'll send the steam straight to your inbox,
starting with a deliciously naughty story:

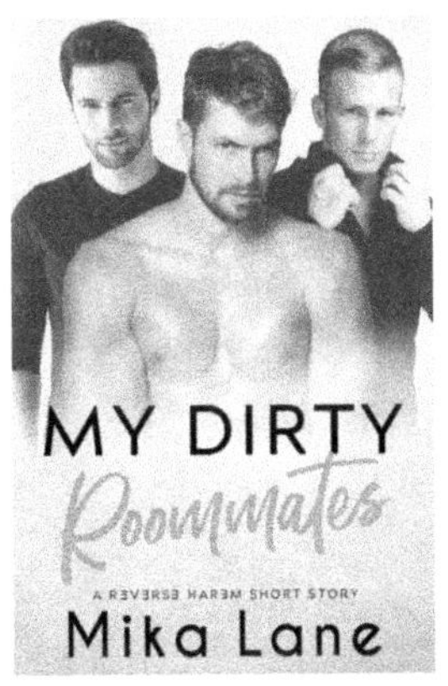

SIGN UP TO MY MAILING LIST!
Or visit:
https://geni.us/free-book-signup

SHOP
Mika
Lane

KEALY

Smack.

"Ouch! I am not a pin cushion."

A skinny creature with the neck of a giraffe twisted away from me, ripping the delicate fabric I was trying to piece together around her skeletal arm right out of my cramped fingers. And if that weren't bad enough, she turned and *smacked my hand.*

Did someone really just *smack my hand?* I hadn't been smacked since I last engaged in some sort of infraction like rolling my eyes or sassing an adult.

The freak of nature who stood before me, said hand smacker, who got paid thousands of dollars to scowl and slink down a runway wearing my fashion designer boss's creations, failed to realized *I* was the one holding the sharp objects. With large sewing shears hanging on a ribbon around my neck and a handful of straight pins between my fingers, I could cripple *her* if she didn't start to show me some respect. Her sharp elbows were no match for my weapons.

Well, straight pins couldn't cripple anyone, but I liked to imagine they could.

Twice a year during New York Fashion Week, my boss, one of the top designers in the world, had a big runway show. And I was one of the many junior designers who were turned into office bitches for a week, doing all the shit work that made a runway show come together perfectly.

The newspapers, magazines, and cable programs that covered the shows only portrayed the pretty side of the production—beautiful men and women sashaying down the catwalk in their perfect hair and makeup, under the best lighting money could buy, and with some of the loudest freaking music you'd ever hear outside of a nightclub.

What the public didn't know, however, was that the shows, which took more work than building the Egyptian pyramids, and cost thousands of dollars, were over in *minutes.*

All that work for ten or fifteen minutes of pomp and circumstance.

If that's the case, why bother? I asked when I was the new girl on Forest's team. And after staring at me like I had two heads, one of the office snots explained it this way: if you *do* show during Fashion Week, you may or may not be noticed (but hopefully you would). And if you didn't, people would draw all manner of conclusions about you, your collection, your business, and your general ability to walk the face of the Earth with your head held high.

So you kind of *had* to show.

Not that my boss minded the incredible burden it put on his staff, nor the money that was sucked out of his coffers. He didn't have to do the shit work, nor did he have to work for a pittance like the rest of us because the company's money went to impressing the editors of *Vogue* and *Elle*, rather than being used to pay us minions. Ah, the benefits of ownership.

But hey, no one forced us to work there. No, we were pretty much complete idiots all on our own.

But at that particular moment, I was a desperate woman. With the start of the show only minutes away, my boss was on the other side of the room shaking hands and air kissing celebrities, fashion press, and other Important People while discretely glancing over his shoulder in my direction. And his look told me all I needed to know. It was on me to make sure the first model supposed to walk in the show was in her outfit and ready to go, no matter what it took. Things were such a scramble in the run-up to a show like ours that regardless of the state the garments were in—open seams needing to be sewn, missing zippers or buttons, it didn't matter—they were still paraded down the runway. All it took was a needle and thread and occasional glue to get them to stay on the bodies showing them off. That left us pinning, sewing, taping, and gluing up to the final minutes.

This 'business as usual practice' was not normally a problem, except that at that moment, I was dealing with the biggest *prima donna* super model on the planet. Translation—*major pain in the ass.* Just days before, the tabloids reported she'd beaten a cab driver over the head with her purse because he dropped her off on the wrong side of the street.

I guess I was lucky I got off with a mere hand slap.

"I'm sorry," I explained to the twig, trying not to choke on my words. That's what those of us in the office who were buddies called the models behind their backs. Twigs. Like Twiggy, that famous model from back in the day.

Anyway, the twig looked down at me as if I were lower than the dirt on the bottom of her shoe. And because I was desperate to get her on the runway, make my boss look good, and keep my job, it was a role I was temporarily willing to play.

"Look at my beautiful girl," my boss cooed as he floated over to us.

The twig rolled her eyes dramatically. "Oh, Forest! It's been such a day. And now look at me. *Just look at me,*" she whined.

Forest and I looked her up and down. If there was something we were supposed to acknowledge, it was lost on me. The woman looked perfect as I pulled one more stitch, knotted my thread for security, and stepped back to let Forest admire his masterpiece.

He stepped in front of me since I'd worked my magic and was no longer needed. He took the twig's hands in his own and leaned close to murmur something in her ear.

Whatever it was, he'd done the right thing, because her face instantly brightened. She was ready to walk, and he led her by the hand to the backstage area where the rest of the models had assembled. In the moments before they were to go on, they looked bored, not to mention hungry, standing there with their arms crossed and chatting amongst themselves.

What did models talk about with each other?

"You're so skinny. Wow."

"Oh no, you're much skinnier. And prettier, too."

"No way, you're prettier..."

And on, and on...

Anyway, I could only guess what they conversed about, because they didn't talk to me, or any of my coworkers, unless they wanted something like a glass of water or a carrot stick to suck on.

Deafening show music began to play as people with headsets ran around like maniacs, and the first set of models marched out onto the runway in Forest's latest designs. I waited where he and the twig had left me—she'd return in moments, and I had to help her into her next outfit. While cooling my heels, I waved across the room at my coworker, Muse, over on the men's side, dealing with male models and their outfits. I envied his job. Working with the guys was a breeze compared to some of the bitches I had to contend with.

My twig returned with a light sheen of perspiration on her forehead, which a deft makeup artist dabbed away. Not to make excuses for her bitchiness, but I knew the runway lights were hot and being sewn into a garment was not exactly comfortable. As soon as she held still, I took my stitch ripper and ran it up the seam I'd just sewn to close her in. With a couple pushes and pulls, I slipped the garment off and helped her step into the next one.

I stood back to make sure she was good to go and nodded. She ran to line up again with her group, shook her head and rolled her shoulders, and plunged into the spotlight.

Since each model was to wear only two outfits, I was pretty much done. I sneaked out the back of the stage to stand unnoticed in the audience and watch the show just like the few hundred guests attending that morning.

The models came marching down the catwalk, first the women and then the men, all wearing the same disinterested expression, which was exactly what Forest wanted. And if Forest was happy, we were all happy.

Twig after twig did that weird runway walk models do where they take longer than natural steps, putting each foot in front of the other to create a funny sway that made them look both awkward and badass at the same time.

Then, the male models came. They had their own weird way of walking, too, where they moved their shoulders back and forth in a pseudo masculine move that no normal man would ever actually use.

But I had to say, as odd as their runway walk was, they

were freaking drop-dead gorgeous. While a lot of the male models were androgynous to the point of actually appearing interchangeable with the women, our shows always used the butchest men Forest could find. Actually, he didn't find any of them. The agency that helped us put on our shows found them. Forest just approved them; a job he relished.

I found an empty seat and settled into it, making sure I was in the shadows where no one could find me. I had to see as many of the outfits as possible come down the catwalk, especially the men's wear ones I had worked on, but I didn't want Forest to think I was slacking. He was actually an awesome guy and great boss, but during the shows, he'd whip himself into an insufferable lather, for which he'd later apologize.

During the last show we had, when we were backstage and the models and guests had all left, he bent over a trashcan and puked his guts up.

Because fashion was glamorous, right?

2

RAND

"Dude, what's up with these trousers?" my buddy Marlon whispered to me.

I looked at what he was wearing and then back at my ensemble.

"I have no fucking idea, but this is some ugly shit," I whispered back.

The trousers we wore had some kind of weird diagonal fly that buttoned across the crotch instead of the standard vertical opening, presumably for great aesthetic fashion effect.

Marlon lowered his voice to make sure no one could hear us. "Did Forest really design this crap? Because if he did, he should have his head examined."

I looked around at the other male models in our small makeshift dressing room. Everyone looked a bit confused about the strange garments, but they were trying to just suck it up.

Yeah, when you modeled in fashion shows, you never knew what the hell they were going to ask you to wear. But they paid us well, so we kept our mouths shut. Unless they wanted us to wear assless chaps.

That's when we would say, *thanks but no thanks.* And that had never happened, anyway.

So pants with weird openings were not the worst things in the world, but it did mean I had to have some 'dresser' help me into them when I would have preferred to dress myself. Luckily, there was only one more change of outfit for this particular show—only one more weird-ass garment I'd have to wear down the runway for all the fashionistas in the audience who'd trip over each other just eating it up. Then, I could get back into my street clothes of tattered jeans, a faded rock 'n roll T-shirt, and a beanie pulled down almost to my eyes. I blended in just like any New York slob once I washed off the nasty makeup they put on my face to cover a couple zits and red spots.

What could I say? Nobody's perfect...right?

And no one passing me on the street would ever guess I'd just made a shitload of money for wearing ugly clothes and walking on a catwalk for five minutes. I almost felt guilty about it.

Almost.

And given where I started in life, it was a freaking miracle I even had a roof over my head, much less a nicely-growing bank account.

"C'mon," Marlon said, nudging me in the back. "We gotta get lined up."

"Yeah, yeah," I said, falling into line with the other guys who'd be walking the runway with us.

Forest, whose ugly clothes we were wearing, was running around like a maniac making sure we were prepped to perfection and that we had every hair in place. The funny thing was, he was going for a bit of a 'grunge' look, so our hair was actually pretty messy. They'd spend hours making it just right, which I found to be pretty ironic.

"Rand," Forest said, tapping my shoulder and turning me so he would give me a once-over. "Handsome as ever, honey," he said and moved on to check over the next model.

I leaned toward Marlon, who was queued up just in front of me. Our other buddies, Shane and Cross, were toward the back of the line looking bored out of their minds.

"Yo, Mar, you got any other shows lined up for this week?" I asked.

He nodded without fully turning around. Right before we went on, they liked us to be quiet.

"I do. I got a busy week. You?" he asked.

"Ugh. My agent is such a dick. He got in a fight with half the designers in town, and now, they don't want to work with him."

At that, Marlon turned fully to face me.

"How long have I been telling you to get rid of that

douchebag?" he asked.

A loud *shhhhh!* came out of nowhere.

He was right. I'd only hesitated to dump my agent because he'd gotten me into the business when I needed some money. But lately, he was on to fresher meat, and if he was burning bridges, that meant I was going to pay the price.

A little sprite of a guy wearing a headset and holding a clipboard was speaking quietly into his mic and doing a countdown with the fingers on one of his hands.

"Dude, after this show, I'm taking you right over to meet with my agent. He's gonna love you," Marlon said.

With that, Marlon was tapped on the shoulder by the sprite. He walked past the curtain separating the back stage area, made a sharp right, and was gone from my view. After a ten-second interval, a hand on the shoulder let me know I was up. I turned the corner, walking into the blinding lights.

I stomped down the runway in the strange, militaristic-walk they'd asked of us, in time to the blasting music. I passed Marlon on his way off the catwalk, and then, I was on my own. Camera flashes went off, but I pretended not to notice them. I just kept my disinterested scowl on and stomped *left, right, left right,* until I was at the end of the runway, where I pivoted to head back and give everyone one last look at Forest's latest creation. From the applause, he must have done something right. They were eating it up.

Just before I passed the next guy coming out, I caught

sight of a woman in the audience, sitting against the wall, watching the show. While I had only a split-second to register, she was the cute blonde I'd seen running around backstage with the female models before they'd gone on.

She was beautiful, sure, but what had got my attention, I suppose, was the graceful way she handled the pre-show chaos.

Before I knew it, I was off the stage and rushing back to my next outfit change. Marlon, just steps ahead of me, was already dressed and ready to go. A dresser unbuttoned my clothes, which I stepped out of as quickly as I could—he had the next shirt over my head and in moments, I was re-dressed and once again in line behind Marlon. Shane and Cross were still being fussed over when a hairdresser checked me and a makeup artist dabbed something across my forehead, presumably to absorb the sheen of sweat I always got from the goddamn boiling lights.

"Whatcha doing tonight?" Marlon mumbled out of the corner of his mouth.

"Eh, I gotta get some studying in. I got a history exam coming up."

"Cool. You liking your classes?" he asked.

Did I like my classes? Did a bear shit in the woods? I freaking loved everything about City College, from its dumpy campus to its brilliant teachers, and everything in between.

No one ever expected me to go to college, especially me. It hadn't crossed my mind, nor the minds of anyone in the family I grew up in. It just wasn't done. I'd never even known anyone who'd even *been* to college aside from the teachers I had in grade school. But modeling, which I fell into in a completely accidental way, broadened my horizons and made me believe the key to upward mobility—at least mine, anyway—would be to get a degree under my belt. It was great for paying the bills and even building a nest egg, but it wasn't a long-term thing. Not for me, nor for anybody, really.

I passed Marlon again as I entered the runway and he stomped off. The blonde was gone, probably to get back to work, and I was backstage again before I knew it. We had to wait around for a few minutes while Forest walked out on the stage and bowed, making his little speech, thanking everyone for contributing to his latest collection. We'd run out and surround him with even more applause while he took several deep bows to the audience.

It was an odd ritual, but then, fashion was a strange game, anyway.

For example, the model who'd been loudly bitching out the pretty blonde earlier? I watched as she popped a pill into her mouth and chased it down with a bottle of water.

Guess she wouldn't be eating the rest of the day.

3

KEALY

HAD SOMEONE JUST PUNCHED ME IN THE STOMACH?

Because it sure felt like it.

The show had come off without a hitch, in part because people like me worked our asses off around the clock in the days leading up to the event. Even better, Forest's latest collection was met with raucous cheers and applause. I was thrilled for him, for me, for the whole company. He'd be all over the style pages for days, just like he always was. The press, celebrities, big shots from the luxury stores—they all loved him.

And during the brief interlude when I'd sneaked into the audience, I'd had the chance to see a couple of the men's outfits presented by our gorgeous male models. Forest had a talent for choosing guys who would make his clothes look awesome. Today was no exception.

The mood for this show was on the rough and tumble side, with the guys walking the runway with mean-ish scowls, messy hair, and an almost violent *stomp, stomp* of their feet. In any other setting, it would have looked like cheesy over-acting, but in the context of a short fashion show, when you had only minutes to make an impression, it somehow worked.

What didn't work for me, however, were the models who threw their clothes on the floor when they were changing back into their jeans and T-shirts. What the hell?

Anyway, I turned my ear to listen to Forest being interviewed by someone from *Women's Wear*.

"Forest, you knocked it out of the park, again, with this fabulous new collection. How do you do it? What is your secret?" the reporter asked.

Forest looked in my direction with a grateful smile and held his hand for me to join him.

My heart started to pound. I'd never spoken to a reporter before. And cripes, I looked like shit because I'd been up almost all night and had been running all day. But he didn't seem to have a camera with him, so maybe I could just say something brilliant and those who later read my words would just assume I was as gorgeous as the model who'd just stepped on a pile of clothing in her hurry to get out of the place.

But at that moment in time, the bitchy, slobby models meant nothing to me. If their haughty attitudes were the price to pay for our—well, *Forest's* success—then I could stomach a little humiliation. I hustled over to my boss and

Women's Wear, quickly organizing my thoughts about what had inspired the season's collection and what we thought it meant to the fashion world at large.

I mean, what *Forest* thought it meant to the fashion world at large.

Anyway.

I put my hand in his open one, and I saw tears in his eyes. That gave way to a bit of wateriness in my own. I took a deep breath and readied myself for the reporter's first question.

But for some reason, he just kept looking right at my boss.

Like I wasn't even there.

"Forest, the fabrics you chose for this season were beyond sumptuous. Can you tell us a bit about them?"

"Well, we started by traveling to the far corners of the Earth to see what cottage industries—you know, tiny little villages and such—were able to produce. We came across the most beautiful silks and woolens I'd seen in my entire career when we were in India and Pakistan. I mean to tell you, I nearly cried with joy when we found these scarce treasures…"

Forest continued clasping my fingers while he told his story. I stood there with an idiotic smile on my face, nodding politely to back up his bullshit story about traveling halfway around the world—the furthest *he* ever ventured was to Fire Island in the summer—while I patiently waited my turn. When he paused to take a breath, I cleared my throat and prepared to jump in.

But I wasn't fast enough.

"And Forest, where did your inspiration for the unique diagonal opening on the men's trouser come from? I mean, it looked like something that might have come from Napoleon's era. I love how you embraced that rather than designing the pant with the typical vertical fly zipper."

Okay then. They'd called out the most unique design detail of the whole show, and *this* was what I was prepared to comment on.

My brainchild. My baby.

"Well, thank you for your kind words—" I started, ready to explain why I'd added this particular flourish.

But Forest beat me to it. Again.

"The credit for that, my friend," he said to the reporter, "goes to my assistant designer right here—"

I loved that man and the way he was cool about sharing credit.

"Muse? Muse? Are you still here?" he called over the racks of clothes.

What? Why was he calling my coworker Muse?

"Oh, hey boss," Muse sang out as he skipped toward us with a huge grin, his signature bowtie slightly cock-eyed.

"Muse, this is the reporter from Women's Wear, and he wants to hear about the origin of the diagonal buttoning on our trousers," Forest said, throwing his free arm around Muse's shoulders.

Something like confusion and then anger, roared through my head. If Muse had answered the question, I hadn't heard him. *What the fucking fuck* was screaming through my brain like a goddamn broken record. I wanted to wrest my fingers out of Forest's grip but he was squeezing them so tightly, my hand hurt.

But Muse blathered on, and Forest watched him with adoring eyes. It was as if I wasn't even there.

He must have said something funny, because Forest finally released my hand to bring his to his forehead to feign something scandalous being said.

That was my opportunity to escape, which I did with great speed. I ran to the other side of the backstage area and lowered myself to the floor in between a couple rolling racks. And it just so happened that hanging right in front of me were all the trousers with the diagonal openings. Yes, the design detail Muse and Forest were gushing about with the reporter I'd just run away from.

The design detail that *I* had developed.

Not Muse.

Not Forest.

Me.

I WASN'T sure how long I sat there, hiding among the trousers like a little kid—the fucking trousers that *I* had designed, the wool for which had *not* come from halfway around the world but rather, one of the dusty Chinese fabric showrooms in Midtown.

Oh god, oh god, oh god.

Devastated. That's what I was. Muse was my *friend*. Forest was my *hero*.

My belief system, such as it was, shattered. Demolished, really, by two of the people I cared about most. Where the fuck do you go from there?

When I emerged from my hiding place—I couldn't be a petulant, sore loser forever—I straightened my cramping legs and found the reporter gone. Forest and Muse were chatting like old friends.

Maybe they were sleeping together? Nah, Muse wasn't Forest's type. He preferred big, hairy guys, and Muse looked like he'd blow away in a stiff wind.

Plus, he wore bowties.

"Kealy. I wondered where you'd run off to," Forest said. "Hey, can you pack up those dresses over there?" he asked, pointing to a pile I'd seen at least two of the twigs stomp on with their dirty black boots.

"Um…yes, of course…Forest. Hey, Forest, do you think I could talk to you for a sec?" I asked, picking up armfuls of soiled dresses. Thank goodness we had another set of samples, because these were pretty much trashed.

Muse stood there with his usual impish grin, making no move to either help pick things up or leave Forest and me to talk.

Forest approached me. "What's up, Keal? What's on your mind?"

I glanced over his shoulder at Muse, who was still watching with great interest. "Muse," I said, "can you give us a minute?"

His smiled dissolved into a scowl as he slunk away.

"Forest," I said. No point beating around the bush. "Um, Forest, you know when the reporter asked you about the collection's trousers? And the inspiration for them?" I asked.

"Yes, I do." He was still glowing from the show excitement.

C'mon Kealy. Put on your big girl panties.

"Forest, that was my design, not Muse's," I said simply.

He leaned closer as if I hadn't spoken loudly enough.

Maybe I hadn't. So I leaned closer to his ear.

"Forest, those trousers were my design. Not Muse's."

Tilting his head, he furrowed his brow.

"Kealy, I'm not sure what you are saying," he said.

How the hell could I make it clearer?

"Forest, I think Muse is taking credit for my work," I said.

His hands immediately flew up like a stop sign. He took a step back as if I were contagious.

Then he took a deep breath and put an arm around my shoulders the same way he had with Muse to walk me to a corner of the room.

"Kealy, I know you are a hard worker, and you are a wonderful designer. Someday you will do great things," he said.

Wait. What? *Someday I'll do great things?*

"Forest, I can show you my sketches in Illustrator. They'll have date marks—"

His voice grew stern. "Kealy, I'm going to have to ask

you to drop this. I don't need any drama in my company, nor accusations of stealing. I told you, your day *will* come. You are a very talented woman."

He turned and walked away, leaving me standing holding the pile of soiled samples.

But I couldn't see the big, nasty footprints on them.

My eyes were too full of tears.

4

MARLON

Damn if I didn't have to struggle to get out of those stupid trousers Forest had made the centerpiece of his show.

There was just no accounting for taste in this business. If people liked you, they liked your shit. If not, you were screwed. If you were the darling of the fashion press, you were in. If not, forget it. If you had the endorsement of some celeb who wore your threads on the red carpet, well, you were golden. If not, you were pond scum.

Yeah, from what I could tell, fashion was more a popularity contest than anything. Like when you're in high school—there was an "in" group, and everyone outside it watched from the sidelines.

But hey, who was I to be biting the hand that fed me? I mean, my silly little modeling gigs paid my expenses and then some. Actually, I had enough left over to live pretty well. In New York City, that's saying something, where half the inhabitants were scraping by on a daily basis.

"Marlon. How are you?"

Whose sultry voice was that?

I zipped myself into my jeans and whipped around to find one of the female models, still in her weird runway outfit, standing right behind me.

And when I say right behind me, I mean almost on top of me. I had to take half a step back so my eyes could focus on her.

"Oh, hey, Linny is it?"

She looked like a Linny. Maybe because it rhymed with skinny.

Running a long finger up my forearm, she tilted her head.

If they gave Academy Awards for coyness, she'd win, hands down.

"Hey, I was wondering if you'd like to, you know, go for a drink or something?" she asked.

She needed something more along the lines of a cheeseburger.

"Um, well, it's only eleven a.m.," I said.

"Oh. Right. Yeah, I guess it's too early for a drink. Coffee, then?"

She continued to stroke my arm, running her finger under the short sleeve of my ratty polo shirt, and then brought her hand up to my shaved head. I really didn't like it when people helped themselves to my head—something that happened to us bald guys all the time.

Dammit.

I didn't want to give her any ideas.

"Maybe some other time, Linny? I've got another show in later today."

"Oh. You do? Okay, then." She pouted and wandered back to where someone waited to help her out of her dress-thing, or whatever it was she was wearing.

If there was one thing I was *not* interested in, it was models. I knew half the dudes in New York wanted nothing more than to cart a model around on their arm, no matter how much money they had to spend on her, and no matter how much of a bitch she was. Beautiful women were currency to some—mostly the kind of guys who needed to buy their self-esteem.

Guys like that wanted their beauties, and the beauties wanted their money. A win-win for both parties. If that was your thing.

It wasn't mine, though. That was for damn sure.

No, I liked women with a bit of meat on their bones, and given the choice, actually more than just a bit. I liked some healthy curves on a girl who I could take out to a nice dinner, who'd actually eat the food on her plate. Yeah, that was my thing.

"Yo, you off to another show?" Rand asked me

"Yeah, I gotta hit the road. See you guys tonight?" I looked a couple rows over, and our buddies Shane and

Cross were struggling to get out of their pants, just as I had.

Rand followed my gaze. "I know, what the hell was up with those pants?" he whispered after making sure Forest wasn't in the vicinity.

"Who the hell knows? But I'll tell ya, I overheard him being interviewed and the reporter was just about creaming his jeans over them," I said quietly.

"Well, good for him," Rand said. "Forest sells his clothes…we keep getting asked back for his shows."

"Hey, who is that blonde woman over there?" I asked, craning my neck over the racks of clothes.

"Hey fellas, what's up?" Shane asked, changed back into his street clothes.

"Marlon's checking out the tall girl over there," Rand said, gesturing with his chin.

Which led to Shane craning his neck to see what the fuss was all about.

"Guys, could you be a little discrete, please? Christ almighty," I said, ducking my head.

"Oh, relax, asshole," Shane said, continuing to look. He'd always said that if an Irishman wasn't swearing at you, he didn't like you. "Which tall girl? They're all tall."

Rand bent to grab his backpack and hoisted it over his shoulder. "The one who *isn't* a model."

"Oh, that one." He turned back to us and pointed at Rand's pack. "What the hell is in there, Rand? Fifty pounds of bricks?"

"Yah. More like fifty pounds of books. I've got a test to study for, my friend."

"Get to it, Rand." I slapped him on the back.

"Hey, guys, we still getting together for drinks tonight?" Cross, always the slowest to get back into his street clothes, asked.

"You get a sitter?" I asked him.

"No, Marlon. I was going to strap Joey to my back and keep him out 'til all hours of the morning."

"Shit, Cross. Calm down," I said.

He took a glance at his watch. "Speaking of which, I gotta go home and meet my little guy for lunch."

"Ha, Cross. Joey's already cooking?" I asked.

"No, jerk. The sitter makes us lunch. I just hang out with my man."

"C'mon, Cross," Rand said. "I'll walk to the subway with you."

"See you guys tonight."

That left Shane and me.

"Anyway, Shane, do you know the blonde? You're always flirting with the girls at these things."

"Eh, they just like my Irish accent, is all. The minute they find out what a prick I am, they head for the hills."

"As they should."

Shane might not have been the best-looking guy in the room with his wiry red hair and crooked nose, but his unique look opened all kinds of doors in a modeling world that was always looking for something new and different. And his Irish charm got him laid more than anyone else I knew. I mean, the guy quoted poetry by freaking William Butler Yeats.

You couldn't compete with that.

"Well?" Shane asked.

"Well what?"

"Are you gonna stand there all day like a loser, or go talk to the girl?"

"Shut up, will you?" I asked.

"Hey, guys, you almost done here?"

Shit, the pretty blonde was right in front of us, gathering up the sample garments to go back to their office.

Of course, Shane took the opportunity to humiliate the hell out of me.

"Well, looky who we have here," Shane said, laying on his famous charm.

Startled, she looked around to make sure we were talking to her and not someone else.

"Huh? Oh, hi," she said.

Now that I could see her close up, her eyes were a little red. What did she have going on?

She stopped picking up clothes long enough to put her hand on her hip and check out the crazy Irishman.

"You're Shane, right? From Ireland?" she asked.

I rolled my eyes. The girls really did love him.

"Yes, young lady, I am Shane from Ireland. And my friend here is Marlon from America."

She smiled but was not overly impressed. I liked that.

I took the opportunity to extend my hand.

"Marlon. From America," I said.

"Well, hi. I'm Kealy. Also from America. I've seen you at our shows before, too."

I couldn't tell you what it was, but when she took my hand, it was like someone had turned the heat up in the room. I had to either get out of there or pull on my cap before my bald head began to drip sweat.

Kealy's gaze moved over my shoulder, and I turned to see Shane high-tailing it out of the place.

He was cool that way.

"So, you work for Forest?" I asked.

Ugh. What a dumb question to ask. But I was so damn distracted by her glittery green eyes, even if they were rimmed in a little red. I didn't think I'd ever seen anything quite like them.

She nodded, too polite to acknowledge my nervousness.

Why the hell was I nervous? New York was full of beautiful women. I talked to them all the time.

But there was something about this one. And I was going to find out what it was.

5

KEALY

I WAS GOING TO KILL THAT LITTLE WEASEL, MUSE. TAKING credit for my work?

Not on my fucking watch.

I didn't know yet how I would prove those designs were mine, but I'd find out how he'd made Forest think they were his and set everyone straight. The nerve of that little fucker.

He'd been so nice to me when I'd started.

"Hey, you're the new girl," he'd said, looking up at me as I walked in one morning. A lot of people had to look up at me.

"Hey. Nice to meet you," I said, happy to talk to someone friendly. "How long have you been here?"

He looked just like the New York fashion guys I'd gone to school with—super straight-legged pants, a bowtie with their shirts, and heavy nerd glasses. Hair longer in the front, nearly hanging in the eyes, with a streak of some rainbow color. Quite adorable, really.

"Been here two years. It's a lot of fun, and Forest is a great guy. He really encourages you to try things. Some head designers only let the juniors do the shit work like make patterns and stuff."

He followed me to my desk as I turned on my iMac. " Whatcha working on?" he asked, looking over my shoulder.

I was flattered he was interested. That was my first mistake.

"Oh, I'm just playing around. Ya know. I'm not that busy at the moment," I said, pulling up some sketches in Illustrator.

Muse studied my line drawings. "They're good. Forest will like them, too. Hey, some of us are going for drinks after work today, if you'd like to join?"

Hell, yeah. I didn't know many people in New York aside from the family I'd nannied for. Between taking classes and looking after their kids, I'd barely had a moment of rest the last three years, never mind the time to hang out with friends.

And that was how it started, my brief and ill-fated friendship with Muse. I was thrilled to have a new friend. He took me all over town, introduced me to his friends, helped me get cooler clothes, and showed me the places to hang out. He was the perfect coworker and buddy.

Until he wasn't.

I'd grown up around a lot of less than desirable people, so I should have smelled a rat when Muse was so over-the-top nice to me. But I'd figured any ugly part of my life was behind me then and that I was finally meeting the kind of people I wanted to be around.

I hadn't known many decent folks until the Benson family hired me for childcare, and I'd certainly never known anybody like them. They welcomed me into their home like I was family, and eventually had me move in to be their full-time nanny. They're the ones credited with helping me go to design school.

Yeah, my new life in New York was a completely different universe from the one I had growing up. Thank goodness, because the path I'd been on was not survivable.

WHEN I'D FINALLY FINISHED GETTING ALL the shit needed for the fashion show packed up and back to the office, because of course, Muse took off, leaving all the work to me, I immediately called my roommate.

"Hey, Keely," she said. "How was the show? Is it over?"

"Ohmygod, Fantine." I'd slipped into the conference room for some privacy.

"What? What the hell happened?"

"You know that guy Muse I work with?"

"Yeah. The one who came to our Christmas party? Who wears the bowties?"

I wanted to take one of those stupid bowties and

strangle him with it. "Yeah, him. Well, he stole one of my designs."

"What the hell? How can that happen?" she asked.

Too easily, because I was a sucker for someone who was nice to me. "Well, we were all working on our new designs for this season's collection, and he convinced my boss that he'd come up with the new trouser that I freaking slaved over."

The noise of the city roared in the background, nearly drowning out Fantine's voice. Okay, look. We can handle this. Just go talk to Forest. You've always said he was a good boss. I'm sure he'll listen."

"I already did say something to him, at the fashion show. He shut me right down. I couldn't believe it." Just talking about it got my heart pounding.

Actually, I didn't know which was worse—Muse fucking me over, or Forest not believing me.

"No way, really? Hey, sweetie, I'm running into an audition. I'll catch you later at home, okay?"

I slunk back to my desk. No one had heard my conversation in the privacy of the conference room, but because it was all glass, everyone had seen me in there. It was where people went when they had something personal to discuss. So it was kind of private but not.

Shit. Muse was side-eyeing me. Probably wondering if I was going to kick his ass.

I was so tired from the show, and so upset with Muse and Forest, I left work early. I didn't even tell anyone.

When I got home, I undressed to my skivvies and

hopped in bed. Sometimes, that was all I could do, and this was one of those times.

"KEALY, WAKE UP."

I opened my eyes to a dark room, where I could just make out Fantine.

"What are you doing in bed so early? It's only six o'clock," she said.

I reached through the fog in my head for my nightstand light. Switching it on made me squint. "Wow. I just laid down for a little nap. Guess I was really tired."

Fantine scooted up on the bed next to me and propped a pillow behind her back.

"I brought home some of your favorite Thai. I thought it might make you feel better," she said.

I had a lot of things to be grateful for, and at the top of the list was Fantine. She was always looking out for me.

"Oh, thank you. You're the best." I leaned over and kissed her cheek. "Hey, how was the audition?"

Fantine was always going from one audition to another for various off and on-Broadway shows. She got a few parts here and there, but I had to hand it her—she never got discouraged. She believed auditioning was a numbers game and that if she tried out for enough parts, she'd eventually get something big.

"It was good. They had me sing that stupid song from

Cats. Everyone wants to hear the song from *Cats*. I'm so over it."

"I'm starving," I said.

"Good, because I got a ton of food."

Not two minutes later, we were sitting on the floor of our tiny New York apartment, shoveling steamy, spicy food into our mouths.

"You know, Keal, I've seen worse than what Muse did to you."

Well, I had too. But I wasn't going to share that with her. "Yeah?"

"You should see some of the shit that goes down in the theater world. You know how many times I've been asked to get on my knees and give someone a blow job?"

"*What?*"

"I'm serious. It's common. Happens all the time. I won't do it, though. I don't want to be someone who finally 'makes it' and has to live with what I did to get there. No, I'm going to get ahead on my talent."

Fantine could afford to take her time with her career. Her parents paid her freaking rent.

"In fact, just last week, I walked in on a guy giving a producer a blow job. I guess one of the good things about theater is that there are so many gay guys that a lot of them aren't interested in anything from me. Small miracles," she said, shrugging.

I sighed long and loud. "Well, there was one bright light in my day…"

She set her plate on the floor next and turned to face me. "Yeah? Fill me in."

"Well, you know how Forest does both men's and women's apparel?"

"Yeah, I do." She looked like I was going to tell her I'd won the lottery.

Maybe I had.

"Well, most of the male models are kind of creepy and skinny, but Forest is pretty good at picking the manly ones. And there were some hotties there today. I met this guy named Marlon who was very sweet, and freaking hot. Shaved head, rich brown skin, and muscles to die for. You don't usually see models like that. Not at fashion shows, anyway."

Fantine studied me. As carefully as I knew she was choosing her words, I pretty much knew what was going to come out of her mouth.

"You know, Keal, it might be nice for you to get out there again. Go on a date or two."

Easy for her to say. Lush black curls tumbled down her back, the perfect contrast to her bright blue eyes. And she had a flawless hourglass figure. Wherever we went, guys fell at her feet.

Not that I did that badly with the guys—I just didn't have any game. I totally sucked at small talk.

I nodded. "I know. It's been months since the asshole blew me off," I said, trying not to remember how I'd waited a month to sleep with the guy, thinking I was playing it the right way. But apparently, I hadn't, because he completely ghosted me right after I gave it up.

I mean, I'd even met the asshole's mother.

"Are you gonna see him again? Like at a show or something?"

"Well, I know he has to come by the office for a fitting soon," I said.

A slow smile crept across her face. "Now you're talking, my friend. We're gonna cheer you up and figure out how to handle that dickwad, Muse."

"That's what I'm counting on. I really am, Fantine."

6

SHANE

"Christ, what is that smell?" Marlon moaned.

Huh? I lifted my underarm for a whiff and nearly passed out, myself. Damn, that was bad. I slid into the booth beside him, anyway.

"Sorry, lads, I played a raucous game of ball at the community center tonight. Guess I should have taken a shower before I left."

I stuffed my basketball between Marlon and me to give him some distance. Figured it was the least I could do.

Cross craned his neck, sniffing the air. "Whoa. Now I can smell that, too. Christ, Shane, did you just run ten marathons and not shower for a year?"

"Oh, would you whiny bitches shut the hell up. Good lord, you act like I haven't showered in weeks." Seriously. Americans were such sissies about cleanliness.

Marlon scooted as far away from me as he could. The asshole.

"Dude, you are rank. Don't get any closer," he said.

On the other side of the table, Cross grinned at Marlon's disgust.

"Go ahead and laugh," he said. "You're far enough away to escape the real stench."

I was shaking, I was laughing so hard. Okay, yeah, I'd not showered after playing basketball, but c'mon. How bad could it be?

Time to change the subject. I ordered us all a round of beers and some of those disgusting nacho things Americans love so much. I thought that might serve as a nice peace offering to kick the night off in our favorite dive bar.

"So what'd you guys think of the show this morning?" I asked.

Cross shrugged. As long as he got paid, he didn't care what they made him wear, or who he wore it for. He'd probably model a woman's evening dress if it earned him an easy thousand bucks. The priority in his life was bringing up his two-year-old. Marlon, on the other hand, was more particular.

"You know, some of Forest's designs rock. But those trousers today." He shook his head. "But it's not like we have to ever wear them again, though, right?"

"Why don't you just chill, dude? Wear the fucking clothes, walk down the fucking runway, and keep your fucking mouth shut," Cross said, pointing at Marlon.

I took a big swig of my beer. It was just the ticket after a hot, sweaty ball game. Body odor be damned.

"Yeah, Mar. Why you looking a gift horse in the mouth? It's easy money, especially for a college dropout like yourself." I knew just how to goad him. Plus, my Irish accent allowed me to get away with massive amounts of shit.

Rolling his eyes, Marlon ran his hand over his shiny head, which was starting to take on a sheen from the overheated bar.

"Hey, speaking of college boys," Cross said as Rand arrived, falling into the booth next to him. He shoved his weighty backpack under the table, where landed on my sneaker-covered foot.

"Hey, guys," Rand said, pulling his shoulder length hair back with a rubber band while I waved the waitress over for another round of beers.

"How was class today?" Marlon asked.

We might have given Rand shit about being a schoolboy from time to time, but the truth was, we were seriously proud of the bastard.

He nodded slowly as a smile beamed over his face.

"Good, man. Really good." He just looked at the bubbles rising in his beer. "I can't believe I'm doing this. It just rocks."

Cross cuffed Rand's shoulder. "Dude. I know what *that* means. You got another fucking *A*, didn't you?"

He laughed, and his face turned bright red. I liked to see him happy. Hell, I liked to see all my friends happy. But

Rand really deserved it. He'd been through some shit. Had come a long way from the Bronx.

Marlon held his beer up. "I'd like to toast my big-brained friend, here," he said with a laugh, followed by a chorus of *cheers*.

"Yup. I got an *A*. Who would have ever believed that *I* would get an *A* in college history? Fucking amazing."

"Well, congrats, my friend," I said.

He gave me a modest smile. "Hey, speaking of life being amazing, how's Joey?"

Cross's face brightened enough to light the entire room. Actually, the entire city block. That's how much he loved his little guy.

"He's awesome. Just so incredible. If I do say so myself. Running around, getting into everything." Cross smiled and shook his head. "Just like I used to. Wish his mom were around to enjoy it."

The table went quiet for a minute as we all picked at our beer labels.

"Yeah, we know you wish she were still around," Marlon said.

Time to discuss something more upbeat, and being the court jester I was, I stepped up.

"Guys. Marlon was scoping out a lovely lady at this morning's show." How I loved teasing him.

"And how did that go, Mar?" Cross teased. "Wait, who was it?"

Marlon rolled his eyes and looked to the other side of the bar like we weren't there. But it wasn't that easy to ignore us when we wanted to be assholes. Actually, it was pretty much impossible.

"Well, since Marlon won't tell you, I will. It was the beautiful blonde who works for Forest. She was running around like a madwoman as she does at all the shows, but it's impossible to miss her. A mop of messy blonde hair and these pretty green eyes you can see from across the room." I looked at my friend, and he just smiled.

"Yeah, Shane's right. And I did chat her up. Her name's Kealy. She's cool," Marlon said.

Rand shook at finger at no one in particular. "I know who you're talking about. She's gorgeous. What does she do for Forest?"

All heads looked in Marlon's direction, since he was the one who got the skinny.

"She's a junior designer or something like that. But from what I saw at this morning's show, she does a lot of shit work, too," he said. "Kind of kept the whole show together."

Cross looked at his watch. "I can't stay much longer, I gotta get back to the sitter. But Marlon, keep us posted. I think she might be just our type." He said his goodbyes and headed out.

Rand leaned across the table and sniffed deeply. "God, Shane, is that smell you?"

Marlon burst out laughing. And I laughed with him.

"Yup. You guys are being treated to my post-workout stench. And I sincerely hope you are enjoying it," I said. "I'll bring more next time.

Rand turned his nose up and leaned as far back in the booth as he could to get away from me. What a bunch of pussies.

"Speaking of working out, how's the community center?" he asked me.

"It's great. The kids are great. The coaching is great. It's good stuff. Very healing," I said, rubbing the raised scar on my chest.

"Yeah? Do they know you're a sissy boy model in your real job?" Marlon laughed.

"Hey, you should talk. Does your dad know what you do?" I asked.

He smirked and nodded. "He does know. Good old Dad, with a son who's a male model. That just about put him in an early grave."

I laughed. "I bet it did. Bigshot NFL team owner's son wears makeup and prances around in weird clothes."

Marlon nodded. "Yup. That about sums it up."

"So Mar, what's next with the lovely Kealy?" I asked. I hated to be pushy, but I couldn't get the woman off my mind.

"Well, I'll be at Forest's studio for a fitting in the next few days, if I remember correctly. So, we'll see," he said.

"Okay, well work it. We're counting on you," I said.

He leaned back and smiled. "Have I ever let you down before?"

He was right. The last time we shared a woman had been pretty freaking awesome. I couldn't wait to do it again. God, it got me going.

Speaking of going, the three of us still at the bar had stayed well past our bedtimes. We paid the bill and waited on the sidewalk in front of the bar for an Uber ride. Well, Rand and Marlon did. I was close enough to walk.

"You sure you don't want to ride with us?" Marlon asked.

Bouncing my basketball on the ground before me, I waffled, but only for a moment. I wasn't going to be dissuaded from walking around my city.

"No thanks, guys. I want to walk home. Get some fresh air after that stuffy bar. It'll help me sleep."

"You sure?" Rand asked.

The guys knew me well. Their Uber arrived, and they hopped in.

Marlon rolled the window down before they drove off.

"Be careful, will you?" he urged.

I nodded and turned in the direction of home, rubbing the scar on my chest as if that would make it go away.

7

KEALY

MY HAND SHOOK AS I POURED MYSELF A CUP OF LOUSY BREAK room coffee.

I'd never really had a bad attitude about work. I mean, sure, things irritated me every now and again, but the situation was different now. After I'd eaten too much Thai with Fantine the night before, I'd tossed and turned until the sun came up. Aside from the nap I'd stolen that afternoon, I was running on less than empty—I hadn't slept the night before last night either, thanks to preparations for the fashion show.

That's how I ended up on my second cup of nasty, bitter, full-strength coffee. I tried to cut the awful tang with a ton of sugar, but it barely dented the offensive taste.

"Kealy, is that a fresh pot of coffee? I think I'll have

some," Forest said cheerfully, joining me in the break room and pouring some into an *I Love New York* mug.

"Hey, Forest, do you think we could talk for a few minutes?" I asked.

"Sure, Keals."

Usually, I loved his nickname for me, but that day it was like nails on a chalkboard.

"What's on your mind?"

There was no one else in the break room, but I couldn't risk the office gossip if someone were to overhear me. I generally liked the people I worked with, but they'd be all up in my business if I allowed them.

"Um, do you think we could go into the conference room?" People would still be able to see us, like always, but at least they couldn't hear. Forest's office wouldn't do because it was in an open loft that overlooked the rest of the studio. Plus, people ran in and out of there all day long. I wouldn't be able to have a decent discussion with someone interrupting us every few minutes.

"Lead they way, then," he said, gesturing toward the break room door.

When we were in the conference room, I sat at the big table. Forest followed, leaning back in his chair, sipping the crummy coffee.

"What's on your mind today?" he asked kindly.

I really did adore the man. But I had to set the record straight on one thing.

"Thanks for being willing to chat, Forest. I wanted to continue with what I mentioned at the show yesterday."

I had my fingers crossed he'd react positively.

Instead, he frowned, confusion. "Whatcha talking about, Keals?" he asked with concern.

Did he seriously not remember the one thing that, for me, would define my entire year, if not my entire decade?

Holy shit. I was suffering to beat the band, and he was still walking on clouds from a successful show.

Life was so freaking unfair.

"The men's trousers that were such a hit at the show. Forest, I know you think Muse designed them, but he didn't. It was me—"

He held his hand up like a *stop* sign. Shit, that didn't feel good.

"Kealy, I don't like drama in my studio, or among my workers." He stood to leave.

No, no, no.

"Forest, you have to believe me. I'm sorry to say it, but Muse stole my design and then took credit for it. Ask him how he came up with it. You'll see." I was shaking, though I wasn't sure if it was from anger or fright. Or both.

"Kealy, I'd appreciate your dropping this. You are a great employee and on your way to becoming a great designer. Don't cause any trouble for yourself so early in your career. Okay?"

My mouth opened but nothing came out. I picked my coffee up off the table, thinking that if I took a sip, my ability to speak might return. Instead, I dribbled it down my chin and onto my shirt.

Shit.

Forest reached his hand to my shoulder and looked at me. "Sweetie, I like you a lot. I haven't seen many people work as hard as you do. But as you develop, and your work gets better—"

Holy shit, did he really just say that?

"—you'll have the chance to shine, just like Muse did." He moved his hand from my shoulder and put it on his hip while he studied me. "Keep up the good work. I have great faith in you. Okay?"

He turned and left me alone in the conference room where, if it hadn't been like sitting in a fishbowl with half the office staring at me, I would have curled up and broken into tears. The only place I could go to be alone was the ladies' room. I left my coffee and bolted for the least-used stall so I could unload my fury in private.

I was upset about Muse, of course, but Forest not believing me shattered everything I thought I knew about him. He'd always been one of the good guys.

But the truth was, I was never good at picking out the good guys. Or maybe I was just good at picking out the bad guys.

Some things never changed.

"Marina?" I asked.

"Kealy! How's it going, sweetie?" she asked.

The sound of a kind and familiar voice just about brought me to my knees.

"Hi," I said weakly.

"Is something going on? What's wrong?"

I sighed into my cell phone and glanced around the rest room to make sure I was absolutely alone.

"Having some problems at work, Marina. I'm so upset." I choked back a sob.

"Oh, my. Why don't I come meet you at the diner for lunch? Noon good?"

LUNCHTIME COULD NOT HAVE COME FAST ENOUGH, and in fact, it *didn't* come fast enough—I bolted out of the office at eleven-thirty. If I had to sit in our favorite booth and suck down Diet Cokes and fried calamari until I was green around the gills to hold our table, I didn't care. Anywhere was better than at work.

Which made me sad. I loved nothing more than getting up every day and going to work. It didn't matter that the subway was smelly and hot in the summer and soggy with dirty snow slush in the winter. I'd barely noticed those things, to be honest. And when the subway wasn't running at all because of one technical issue or another, I just walked. I couldn't wait to get to the office and see where Forest would lead us that day.

I got paid shit for money, and the hours were long. But those of us in our twenties knew to expect things to be like that. Everyone had a roommate, knew where the dollar beers were each night of the week, and frequented the cheapest Chinese restaurants when we didn't have two nickels left to rub together in the days leading up to payday.

They were good times. I was living the dream. One I'd never known could be mine, given the shitty place where I'd started.

I looked up to see Marina come flying through the diner door, her long black hair waving behind her. Perfect timing. If I had to eat another piece of calamari to hold our table, I might not make it out alive.

"What the hell is going on? I thought you loved your job?" she asked breathlessly. Her office at a big publisher was a few blocks from mine. I knew she was a fast walker, like most New Yorkers, but she must have jogged over, judging by the sweat on her temples.

"Ohmygod. Can I have a sip of your soda?" she asked, grabbing it before I could answer.

When I first met Marina, I called her *Mrs. Benson*. Those days seemed universes away, and yet, they were really only a few quick years. I'd been hired to nanny her three kids. They welcomed me into their family in a way I'd never experienced in all my years growing up in foster care. Before long, I was calling her Marina instead of Mrs. Benson, and she was looking after me like a big sister. I think of those days as the ones when my life really began.

"Hi, Marina," I said, stirring the straw in my soda after she slid it back over the table to me.

She reached for my free hand. "C'mon. I'm here, now. Tell me what's up."

So I shared the story of my supposed friend Muse hijacking my design and the more devastating piece of Forest not believing me.

"Oh, shit," she said. "I don't blame you for being upset.

The waitress came by, and Marina ordered us two giant cheeseburgers and curly fries. She knew exactly what I needed when it came to food.

"You know, Kealy, I believed in you the first moment you walked through my front door. It was just a feeling I had, and it was right. And I still believe in you."

"Thanks, Marina," I sniffed. If it weren't for her belief in me, well, who knew where I'd be. I supposed still providing childcare, not that that was the worst thing, but Marina helped me get into college and then helped me pay for it. But I was going to pay her back some day. It was part of my plan.

"This is what you're gonna do," she said, putting down her burger to let me know she was serious. "You're gonna go back to work, hold your head up, and continue to do kick-ass design. You are going to keep your work to yourself for as long as you absolutely have to before you share it with Forest or anyone else. And you will put this behind you."

"I don't know if I can." One solitary tear dripped onto my half-eaten burger. I knew things were really bad if I couldn't finish my food.

"Keal, you have no choice. Look, you know I've been in publishing for years. In a creative field, people do shitty things. Actually, they do in every field. I've seen it all. And this isn't even the worst you'll see in your career. You're tougher than this. And just think, if Muse had to steal your design, that means he has no ideas of his own. If he can't continue to steal, Forest will eventually see the light."

She waved the waitress over for the check. She always paid, just like the combination fairy godmother/big sister we all wish we had. And were sometimes lucky enough to get.

8

CROSS

A SHRIEK THAT JUST ABOUT SPLIT MY EARDRUMS ERUPTED from beneath the canopy of Joey's stroller. He was going through a phase, as the baby sitter explained to me, where he was "finding his voice."

And from the sound of it, he had a pretty damn loud one, and he was doing a good job of finding it. I rolled his carriage across the sidewalk out of the way of pedestrian traffic to peer under the cover that kept the sun off his face. I had to take a moment to make sure all was well in his world. When your kid sounds like someone's cutting his arm off with a dull knife, and everyone around turns to stare like you're the monster who might be doing it, you tend to check in.

But Joey was fine. In fact, he was better than fine. When

he saw my face, he emitted another shriek, followed by the cutest damn smile I'd ever seen in my life.

How could I be so in love with another human being?

It was just the two of us, Joey and me. We'd lost his mom when he was just a few months old. We were kind of raising each other. Although Joey would not know that for quite a while. No, for now, for all he knew, I was a freaking god. As long as he was fed and had his diapers changed, I pretty much *was* god to him. He was blissfully unaware of my worries about being a competent single parent, serving as a good example, saving money for his college, and the myriad of other items I tried to keep in line on a day-to-day basis.

In fact, it was because of Joey that I was heading to a photo shoot for an ad for Forest's latest collection—the same one my buddies and I had modeled a few days previous in his Fashion Week show.

"Silvana, we're here," I called into the intercom on the outside of the sitter's building. The door buzzed loudly, and I bounced Joey up the front stoop and into the lobby where I called the elevator for the second floor.

"Ah, it's my little *Jose*," Silvana purred, wearing a well-worn apron, her hair pulled back into a tight bun. She grabbed my guy out of his stroller and planted kisses all over his fat little face. He giggled, and all was right in my world. I slipped back out, and neither of them even noticed.

My next stop was the photo studio in Chelsea where all the magic would happen. I'd been there many a time doing catalogue and other modeling gigs, so I knew the drill inside and out. It wasn't the most exciting work, but it paid well and let me work on my mystery novel when there was downtime. And at a photo shoot, there was lots of downtime.

I wouldn't have minded spending all my days spinning yarns, but modeling paid the bills and then some. The choice was a no-brainer as soon as my wife and I had Joey. And now that the kid had only one parent, it was more important than ever to build up a nest egg to protect him in case, god forbid, anything ever happened to me.

"Hi, you're Cross Granville, right?"

Well, damn. If it wasn't the very attractive blonde from the fashion show who we guys had just been talking about. Wait 'til she found out that not one, but four dudes—who happened to be friends—liked her. She'd be thrown for a loop, no doubt—they always were at first. But if she came around, it could be a win-win for everyone.

"Yes, I'm Cross. And you're Kealy, right?"

Her head snapped up from her list, or whatever it was she was looking at, and a blush ran across her face.

"Um, yes. Yes, I'm Kealy."

She couldn't be that surprised I knew her name. Could she? I mean, a pretty girl like that was noticed all the time. Of course her admirers would ask her name.

I extended my hand to put her at ease.

"I'm not a stalker, I swear. I just know your name from Forest's shows." I added my best non-stalker grin.

And it worked. Her hand relaxed into mine, and she

smiled a damn gorgeous smile. The guys had said she had the coolest green eyes, and they weren't kidding. That was the first time I'd seen her up close enough to have a conversation with her, and if there was one thing I promised myself, it wouldn't be the last.

"Why don't you head over there, Cross? Muse will show you what you're wearing and then will get you to makeup. Hey, any particular music you'd like to hear?"

Usually, I was kind of particular about the music played during a shoot, if I were given a choice in the matter. But not that day.

"Why don't you choose, Kealy? I'd like to hear what you like," I said.

And don't you know, she blushed again. Damn, I liked that.

"Okay. I'll choose. Thanks, I never get to pick," she said, heading over to the stereo to get Pandora going.

When I was next up in line for the shoot, I still had some waiting to do but I couldn't sit and relax—the clothes they had me in had been steamed to perfection, and then pinned so they appeared to fit me perfectly. One wrong move, and the whole production team would have to start over. And I'd be in the doghouse.

So I decided to chat up my pretty new friend.

"So, Kealy, which do you enjoy more, fashion shows or photo shoots?" I asked her. Lame question, but I'd never been too good at small talk.

"Oh, definitely the shows. I mean, they are a ton of work, but they're over pretty fast." She looked around to make sure no one was in earshot and lowered her voice. "These shoots take forever, sometimes."

I nodded. "I feel the same way. That's why I bring my laptop. When there's a chunk of time, I'll sit down and do a little writing."

She looked me up and down. "Well, you'd better not sit down right now, or someone will be coming for your head."

I laughed. "I know, I wouldn't dare mess up the perfection that is this ensemble," I said, gesturing over my clothes.

When the shoot was finally over—and by the way, I'd not been able to sit down long enough to write a word of my story, but what are you gonna do?—I took my sweet time getting back into my civvies.

"Hey, Kealy, need any help packing up?" I asked, when I was dressed in my street clothes and had wiped off my makeup.

She looked at me as if I'd just asked her if she was from outer space, which was really no surprise. The models were usually the first to hightail it out of the place once their part of a shoot was over. If she were to do this sort of work until the day she died, she'd probably never get asked that question again, not by a model, anyway. In fact, she was probably going to think I was a psycho stalker. If she didn't already.

"Um, no, I think I've got it under control. I've got my coworker, Muse, over there," she said, gesturing with her chin.

"Well, if you're sure, then I'll head out," I said.

"It was a good shoot. Thank you for coming. I'll see you next time."

Her coworker, the odd little guy wearing a bowtie, was headed in our direction. I wanted to make my move before he cockblocked me.

"Say, Kealy, my friends and I are having a party this weekend. It would be great if you could join us. I think you already know Marlon and Shane. Probably Rand, too."

She nodded. "Yes, I do know them. But, um, I have a lot of work to do this weekend."

"Oh, c'mon. You have to take a break at some point. Bring one of your friends. Bring Mr. Bowtie over there," I said, pointing.

"Yeah, I won't be bringing him," she mumbled.

Oops. Bad suggestion.

"If you're comfortable giving me your number, I'll text you the address."

"Okay." She shrugged. She took my phone and entered her number.

"Great. I hope to see you, Kealy."

"I don't see why not. Unless something comes up," she said.

"Well, if not this time, then another."

But she'd be there. I knew she would.

9

KEALY

"OH, MY GOD, WOULD YOU GET A MOVE ON?" FANTINE hollered from the living room, where she tapped her foot more loudly.

She'd always gotten ready in record time. I, on the other hand suffered from *analysis paralysis*. Simply put, I had too many clothes to choose from. It was both a blessing and a curse. Because I worked in fashion, I either got a good amount of free clothes, or got really good prices on the ones I had to pay for. That was the blessing part. But the curse was, first, that in my tiny, shared New York apartment, I had barely any room to store things, and that second, I had the worst time choosing what to wear.

"C'mon, Fantine, just give me a minute more," I called to her.

Shit, shit, shit. The pile of clothes I'd already tried on

covered my bed and spilled onto the floor, and I was still miles away from making a decision.

Oh, fuck it. I decided to keep on the skinny jeans and booties that I was already wearing and pulled on a little wrap top that really showcased the girls. No such thing as too much boobage when one was going to a party in New York.

"Finally," Fantine sighed when I joined her in the living room.

"Do I look okay?" I asked, twirling.

Fantine herself looked fabulous, like she always did, with her mini dress and over-the-knee boots. Which, I might add, her parents paid for just like they paid her rent. But I didn't hold that against her. She still worked her butt off.

"You look gorgeous," she said, looking me up and down with a smile.

Instant confidence. Fantine was nothing if not painfully honest, and if she approved of my outfit, I knew I was ready to roll.

Just like he'd promised, Cross reached out to me with the details of the party, and not only once; he'd actually checked in a couple times to make sure I had the address and his phone number just in case I needed it. Like if I got lost. Which no one in New York ever did. It was the easiest city in the world to find your way around in thanks to the grid system it was set up on. Avenues running north-south, and streets running east-west. You couldn't go wrong.

So he was clearly contacting me for another reason, which puzzled me until Fantine pointed out the obvious.

"Don't you see, he likes you, you idiot," she said.

Loved being called an idiot by my roommate and now best friend, since Muse had fucked me over. But I carried on.

"Yes, that crossed my mind. I'm just not sure why he'd be interested in *me*. I mean, he's a hunky male model, for heaven's sake."

Fantine rolled her eyes so hard, it must have been hurt.

"Do you not see how beautiful you are?"

Um, no. "Thank you, Fantine. That's sweet of you to say."

"All right. Don't believe me. I don't really care. But I would like to head out while the night is still young." She put her hands on her hips in exasperation. "The Uber is downstairs."

I grabbed for my clutch, one that I'd acquired for pennies at last season's Prada sale.

So, with Fantine and me in the backseat of a Prius, a consistent favorite among Uber drivers, we raced across town to the party Cross and his friends were throwing at Marlon's Soho loft. He must have been doing great, money-wise, because Soho lofts were pretty much *the* place for hip New Yorkers to live, and the competition for them had made prices skyrocket even beyond the usual already-insane New York housing prices.

I'd heard from Muse—back when we were still friends and speaking, and he would dole out the gossip he'd gathered like they were breath mints—that Marlon had come from a wealthy family. So maybe that was the source of his expensive zip code? I wasn't sure. I did know modeling paid well if your agent kept you busy, but the ones who made earnings in the stratosphere, where you could buy things like lofts on Soho, were the few and far between outliers.

Anyway, Marlon's money was not my business. I was just flattered his friend Cross had thought to invite me and my plus-one to their party. I only hoped it wouldn't be full of bitchy twigs like the one I'd recently stuck with a pin. I was on that woman's shit list for sure, most likely for the rest of my life, but I had the petty satisfaction that I'd gotten the last word, so to speak. Or the last prick.

"Why so quiet?" Fantine asked. She looked kind of creepy as the red and green of the changing traffic lights splashed over her pretty face. "Are ya nervous?"

I shrugged and looked out the window, holding on to my clutch more tightly. "Maybe a little."

"Muse won't be there, will he?" she asked.

I whipped my head toward her. "God, I hope not. I mean, I guess he knows those guys from the shows and all, but, he would have told me if he were going."

"I thought you guys weren't speaking."

She was right. He wouldn't have told me if he were going.

Shit.

♦♦♦

OUR UBER PULLED up in front in front of a typical non-descript building with a huge, dented, metal front door. Dents were the usual calling card of an unsuccessful New York burglar. Luckily for the residents of that building, they'd installed an impenetrable door, and said thief was apparently not smart enough to break the lock, either. Such little things were the source of great satisfaction among those of us who loved this city. Thwarting a burglar was almost on par with getting a great rent-controlled apartment or a parking spot in front of your building.

We pressed the buzzer next to *M. Talbot* and were immediately buzzed in without being asked who we were. So much for security.

A rickety elevator was open to the lobby, as if waiting for us. We pressed a button for the top floor, after pulling the cage-like doors together, and the thing began to shudder and shake as it creaked its way through a mechanism that was god-knew how old.

And don't you know, when we reached the top, the elevator opened right into Marlon's apartment. He had the whole freaking floor of the building.

Shit.

Be cool, girl, play it cool.

Fantine skipped in like she owned the place, with her mini dress swinging behind her and her curls bouncing just right. I ran my hand through my signature bleached mop one last time as a kind of security blanket, took a deep breath, and followed her lead. Of course, with the coolest smile I could muster.

"Kealy!" Cross called from across the massive room. To the right was a chef's kitchen that anyone who could make more than a peanut butter sandwich would kill for, and in front of me and to the left was a space so large, I wasn't sure if I should call it a living room or an auditorium.

I looked around at the chic, good-looking crowd—I mean, what else did I expect to see at a party hosted by male models?—and took in Marlon's modern but cozy style. There were several little seating areas to choose from. Some were still empty and some were occupied, but they all had soft and expensive-looking chairs and sofas.

It was like a freaking club.

And then there was a swing in the corner of the room.

A swing.

Cripes, now I'd seen it all. My heart sank a as I thought ahead to the little apartment I'd have to go home to at the end of the evening. I loved what Fantine and I had done with the place, but it was thrift-store chic to be sure, and our main decorations were piles—piles of books, magazines, CDs, and crap like that.

And I'd thought we were doing well.

Cross embraced me in a bear hug that I hadn't been expecting, but that thrilled me nonetheless. Who wouldn't want to be hugged by someone with cheekbones from god and messy blonde hair pulled into a man bun?

And he smelled damn good, too. Something spicy, but also something powdery, like a clean baby just before you dress them.

Funny. A heartthrob smelling like a baby?

"Cross, thank you for inviting me. This is my friend Fantine."

"Fantine. What a cool name. Where's it from?" he asked.

She rolled her eyes like she was all put out, but I knew better. "My father was a huge fan of *Les Miserables*." She loved getting asked that question.

"Ah, Victor Hugo's masterpiece. Gotcha."

Well. He knew literature.

"Hey, why don't I introduce you both to the rest of my posse? Kealy, you've worked with us at the shows, but we've never all hung out together. C'mon," he said.

We followed Cross through the pack, neither of us able to take our eyes off the faded rock 'n roll T-shirt covering his broad shoulders or the low-handing jeans outlining his very muscular ass.

But not watching where you're walking is never a good idea, and I ran smack into another party guest. I was instantly snapped me out of my Cross-induced reverie and almost fell flat on my ass.

And don't you know, who stood before me but my old buddy Muse?

10

RAND

I'D WATCHED THE BEAUTIFUL KEALY ARRIVE AT THE PARTY, and Cross kindly brought her across the room to me and the other guys. She almost fell over the little guy in the bowtie who worked for Forest, but righted herself like nothing ever happened.

"Hey, Rand, I think you know Kealy, and this is her friend Fantine," Cross said.

We all shook hands hello.

"Let me go get the ladies a drink." He headed for the bar.

Holy shit. The two women before me were by far the most beautiful in the entire party, which was full of models and other fashion industry weirdos. But those people were not my tribe. I was in modeling to pay the bills while I was in college, and then I'd be saying *adios* to it all.

And the emaciated models so many guys clamored after?

Well, they could have them.

Kealy and Fantine were the type of women who made my heart pound. Especially the lovely, edgy-looking Kealy from the fashion shows. I could see, although I couldn't tell you how, that she was a woman with a story. Wherever she'd come from, she'd come a long way. And she was still plowing forward.

Just like me.

"I'm glad you ladies could come," I said as Marlon and Shane waved hello from across the room. "Does Marlon's place rock, or what?"

"Oh, my god, I've never see anything like it," Kealy said, incredulous. "It's crazy. I mean, a swing?"

"You know what?" her perky friend said. "I'm gonna go try out that swing right now. See if I don't!" And she marched right over to break the ice with the swing. I'd seen it before. As soon as one person tried it, it would be occupied for the rest of the night.

And now, I could have Kealy to myself, if only for a minute.

"Would you like to grab a seat over here?" I asked, pointing to one of Marlon's cushy velvet sofas.

We settled into a comfy piece of furniture. "I guess modeling's treating Marlon well," she said, sitting back and crossing her legs. She took a tiny sip of her champagne. Smart girl. The night was young.

"Yeah, I'd say so," I said, looking around. I wasn't sure if she knew Marlon's story and how his family was loaded, but it wasn't my place to out my buddy. I tried not to gossip anyway. The industry was bad enough about that sort of thing.

"So, those clothes we wore at Forest's last fashion show were really something, weren't they?" I asked to make conversation.

Her face brightened. "Yes, the trousers were my design." Then just as quickly, her shoulders slumped. She stared at the little bowtied dude on the other side of the room. I couldn't recall his name. And who invited him, anyway?

"Really?" I said. Yeah, I'd be keeping my opinions about those pants to myself.

She leaned closer and lowered her voice. "Well, I designed them, but someone else got credit."

"No way. How did that happen?"

She shook her head slowly. "I'm not entirely sure. But I'll keep my work to myself from now on. I won't be as trusting as I was."

I felt for her, I really did. "Sounds like a hard lesson. But an important one."

She shrugged. "That's true. And that's how I have to look at it. Lesson learned, now move on."

"Well, you want to know something?" I asked. If she was confiding in me, then I'd confide in her.

"Sure. Tell me."

"I'm not sure about those trousers. The fly was just too weird."

She threw her head back and laughed. "Well, thank you

for being honest. I know they weren't for everyone. But they looked nice on you. I saw all you guys on the runway with them."

"Thank you. I appreciate that." Seemed like I'd never get used to being complimented for my modeling. I guess that just showed my discomfort with it and how it would never be a long-term thing for me, anyway.

"I expect I'll keep doing the modeling thing for another year or two while I finish up school." I wanted her to know I wasn't some empty-headed pretty boy. Actually, I wanted everyone to know that.

"Oh, cool, you're taking classes. What are you studying?" I loved that she was interested in something other than fashion. It could be so insular. I hated that about it.

"I'm studying business, but this semester, taking history and math. It's great. No one in my family has ever been to college."

Her eyes widened. "Me, too. Well, at least, I'm assuming I'm the first. I was raised in the foster system."

I'd been right. The woman had a story.

"So you've come a long way, then? Foster kid to top New York designer, to a fancy-schmancy party like this?" I wanted her to know I didn't take any of it too seriously.

She laughed. And damn, if her green eyes didn't glitter in the party's low light.

"What about you?" she asked. "I mean, what's your story? It's not everyday you see a model with pierced ears, covered in tattoos."

"I suppose. I have a colorful past. I was a troubled kid

going nowhere when someone at a shopping mall approached me about working as a model."

"No kidding! I thought that whole idea of being discovered was an urban myth," she said.

"It sounds like it *should* be an urban myth. But when I found out I could make some decent money modeling, I was all over it. The downside is, my father hasn't spoken to me since."

"What? Why?" she asked.

"Well, he's a macho old dude and couldn't stand that one of his sons was doing 'sissy work.' And even now that I have some money saved up, he won't let me help him and my mom. They could really use it. They live in one of the crappiest parts of the Bronx."

"You're from the Bronx? But you have no accent."

Music to my ears… "College will do that to you." Shit, if I leaned over to kiss her right then, would she smack me across the face?

Down boy. Good things come to those…and all that.

"Kealy, glad you could make it." We looked up to see Marlon standing there with Shane.

She popped up to shake their hands. "Thank you so much for having me. That's my girlfriend, Fantine, over there on the swing."

Surrounded by several spellbound men.

"Oh, that's your friend," Shane said. "I was wondering where she came from."

"Yeah, she's with me. I'll keep an eye on her though, don't worry."

Kealy gave us all a sly smile that really made my blood pump, and it was easy to see the other guys had the same reaction. We'd been friends a long time and knew each other pretty damn well. Probably too well.

"Kealy, let me go get you a champagne refill," Marlon said, taking her glass.

"Hey, dude, while you're up, how 'bout another beer for me?" I asked.

Marlon shook his head. "Sorry, Rand, you're on your own. I only get drinks for pretty ladies. And you ain't pretty."

A look of amusement lit Kealy's face, along with a pretty blush. I liked shit like that and felt a little twitch in my pants.

"What do you want to do in the long-term?" I asked Kealy when we were alone again.

She looked around again. She was either paranoid, or there was someone at the party she either didn't like or trust. Maybe both.

"I'd eventually like to have my own men's wear line."

"Really? Cool. Why men's and not women's?" I asked.

"I don't know. I guess I like the fabrications better, the more complex tailoring process. And given how things are going at work, I might need to kick something off sooner rather than later."

"What's keeping you from doing it?" I asked.

"Well, it takes a lot of investment to get a collection together. But I think I know enough people in the industry to make a go of it." She leaned even closer. "I have a sketchbook of designs and am going to start putting together samples soon."

"I'm impressed, Kealy. Damn. You're a go-getter."

"I could say the same about you," she said, smiling.

Shit, now I *really* wanted to kiss her.

I heard a ruckus behind me, and when Kealy looked over my shoulder, she gasped.

"Oh, no. Fantine."

I turned to find Kealy's friend flat on her ass, next to the broken pot of what had been a healthy houseplant moments before she wreaked havoc on it.

"Fantine," Kealy called across the room. She waved too, but I'm not sure Fantine could even see that far. How did someone get that drunk, that fast?

"C'mon, I'll help you get her out of here and into a cab," I said.

"Thanks Rand. I'm so sorry about this."

We each grabbed one of Fantine's arms and hoisted her to her wobbly feet.

"Fantine, what have you done?" Kealy asked, holding Fantine with one hand and trying to pick up the house-plant with the other.

"I don't know, Keal," she replied. "It was just in my way."

"Okay, c'mon. Rand is going to help us out."

Fantine put an arm around each of our shoulders while waving goodbye to everyone. They laughed, of course, because she was so charming. She was the kind of girl who walked into a party and owned it.

Marlon's elevator screeched to the ground floor the

way it always did. I gave him shit about not maintaining it, but he said he liked it loud—he always knew when someone was coming up.

Kealy and I sat Fantine on the stoop while I hailed the first cab that swung by. We gingerly poured Fantine into the back seat, and before Kealy could join her, I placed my hand on her arm.

"I'd like to see you again, Kealy. But I also want to let you know you may hear from the other guys, too."

Now for the tricky part.

"What? What do you mean?" she asked, her faced twisted into confusion.

"Well, we guys like to date the same woman. We call it sharing. You've probably heard of it."

She nodded slowly while she studied me. "I have heard of it. Not sure it's my thing," she said nervously. "I'll stay open-minded, though."

"That's all we ask of you. It's really the only thing we can ask of you."

11

KEALY

"Oh, god. I feel like shit."

"Well, you deserve to feel like shit, Fantine," I said, watching my roommate stumble to the bathroom in her thong panty, her little boobs jiggling as she hugged the wall with two hands.

"Thanks, Keal," she said, slamming the door.

When she emerged, she had her tattered robe wrapped tightly around her. With slitted eyes, she wandered toward me, one hand on the furniture for balance.

I rolled my eyes. "Looking good there, my friend. Hey, I went out earlier. Got you a nice mocha and some donuts. In the kitchen."

She turned up her nose and shuddered, just like I'd hoped she would.

"Do not even say that to me right now. I'm suffering

from the king of hangovers," she moaned, plopping down next to me on the sofa. "What happened last night?"

"You made a mess at Marlon's party, so I poured you into a cab, and we came home."

She smacked her hand to her forehead. "Shit. Oh, shit. I'm sorry. I think I was doing tequila shots."

"You knocked over a huge houseplant. I think it was a fiddle leaf fig or something like that."

"Ugh. It was such a cool party, and I made an ass of myself. Well, I'll send him a new plant. Hopefully, we'll be invited back." She burrowed into the sofa, eyes closed against the bright room.

"Um, *you* might not be invited back, but I think *I* probably will," I said.

Her arm flailed blindly, smacking mine pretty hard. "Oh, shut up. Those guys won't hold it against me. They were cool."

She suddenly bolted upright, ignoring her hangover pain.

"So, did Cross make his moves? I mean, he's the one who invited you, right?"

It was funny how quickly she recovered when there was gossip in the air.

"He did invite me. I mean, us." I gave her my best stink eye. "But what was interesting was that I really spent most of my time with Rand, his buddy."

She frowned. "Oh. That's weird."

"I thought so, too…but I liked him."

"Well, what's Rand's story?" she asked.

"He grew up in the Bronx and was pretty much on a path to nowhere when he was discovered in a shopping mall," I said.

"Get the fuck out."

"I know, right? Like when does that ever happen in real life?"

She shook her head in disbelief, and even in her hungover state, still managed to look beautiful. I kind of hated her for that.

"When he started modeling, his dad all but disowned him. He thinks it's sissy work."

"Ha!" Fantine laughed. "Might be sissy work, but it's not sissy pay."

"Exactly. And he'd like to help his parents out financially, but apparently, his mom's afraid to take any money from him. Thinks the dad will flip."

"Oh. What a sad story. God, I can't imagine my parents doing anything like that."

No, she wouldn't be able to imagine anything like that. For heaven's sake, I don't think I'd ever seen two parents who adored their daughter more than her folks did. They fully supported her struggling actress gig, although they'd recently made noises about winding down the monthly allowance. Something about teaching 'independence' and all that entailed.

"He asked me out."

"He did? But I thought the other guy Cross liked you," she said. Now she was really confused.

Just like I was.

I nodded slowly. "Yeah. I think Cross does like me."

"Oooh. Drama. Cockfights. Wow." She could barely contain her excitement.

"I'm not sure that's how it is."

"What do you mean? They're going to fight over you, I just know it. At least Marlon and Shane are left for me to pick over. They're so hot, and you know Marlon owns that gorgeous apartment…"

Hmmm. How to break it to her?

"I don't think so," I said simply.

"Huh?"

"Well, it seems they're into something they call 'sharing.' Like they all date the same woman." At least, that's what I thought Rand meant.

"Oh."

Was Fantine actually speechless?

"Yeah, I was surprised, too." Actually, I was *still* surprised. Didn't know what to make of it, at all.

"Well, well, well. Looks like our little Kealy might be in for some fun times," she said.

"We'll see. Don't jinx me."

Fantine rubbed her temples dramatically. "Hey, isn't that your phone ringing?" she whined.

She was right. I dashed to my room where I'd dumped my purse the night before and dug for my cell. There was a call coming in from a number I didn't know, but it was the local area code. I took a chance and answered it.

"Hello?"

"Hey, Kealy, it's Marlon. Marlon Talbot."

Holy shit. *Another* one of the guys.

"Oh. Marlon. Hi, how are you?" Shit, was he calling to tell me to pay for the damage Kealy had done to his fiddle leaf fig? Or that we'd never be allowed back over there?

If that were the case, Fantine was really going to get a piece of my mind. She thought she already felt crappy… well, just wait.

"Hey, Marlon, I wanted to apologize for my friend making a mess of your house last night. I'm so sorry." I'd walked back to the living room so Fantine could hear me apologize on her behalf, and so I could make her feel *really* shitty.

"Oh, it was your friend who did that? Ha, I had no idea. Someone cleaned it up right anyway. Probably Cross or someone like that. He's always cleaning things ever since he had a kid."

Cross had a kid? Was that why he smelled like baby powder?

"Yes, that was my friend Fantine." I stuck my tongue out at her. She gave me the finger in return.

"Hey, it's all good. No worries. I was just calling to see if you were free for a late lunch today. I'd call it brunch but that's more Sunday-ish, and today's Saturday."

Okay. Just like Rand had said…

"Kealy? You still there?" he asked.

"Yes, yes, sorry. I um, saw a pigeon on my window sill and got distracted." Okay, that was one of the worst lies I'd ever told.

"Oh, yeah. Pigeons. Anyway, what do you say? Meet me at the Uptown at one o'clock?" he asked.

"Okay," I blurted out. "I'll see you then."

I hadn't even swiped my phone closed when Fantine pounced.

"Who the hell was that? Did you just get asked out? Was it Rand or Cross?"

I had to gather myself before I could speak.

"Neither. It was Marlon, our host from last night. I'm meeting him at the Uptown."

Fantine's mouth dropped open. "Get. The. Fuck. Out."

I nodded, and my thoughts immediately flew to the most important decision I'd make all day.

What was I going to wear?

But I needn't worry about something like that, because my dear roommate, who owed me anyway, sprang into action.

"C'mon. I'm gonna help you get ready."

AN HOUR LATER, Fantine and I had pulled off a casual, low-maintenance look that actually took a hell of a lot of work to accomplish. But thanks to her theater background, she knew all about hair and makeup, and she had a natural knack for pulling together cute outfits. And god knew, I had no shortage of clothes.

"So anyway, if you have lunch with Marlon, will the

other guys be pissed? Rand and Cross? And what was the fourth one's name?" she asked.

I added a bit more lip gloss in case it wore off on the subway ride to the Upper West Side.

"The fourth one is Shane. The Irish guy. And I don't know if they'll be pissed, to be honest. I'm not sure how all this works. You know, it's not like I've done it before."

She pressed a finger to her chin and nodded thoughtfully. "True. That is true. Hmmm." She ushered me to the door. "Text me and let me know how it's going, okay?"

"I might. No promises," I said to torment her. "When you feel better, you might go to the plant store on the corner."

"We'll see. I am gonna chill and see if there's a good movie on. Maybe eat one of those donuts you got."

Oops.

"I hate to break it to you, Fantine. There actually *are* no donuts. I only said that to make you barfy." I tried not to laugh.

A scowl washed over her face, which only made me laugh harder. "You creep. I've been fighting this hangover and am finally feeling better, just so I could have a donut. You're so mean."

She pulled the front door open and mock pushed me into the hallway. She threw her head back, probably just as she'd done in some play or another.

"Get out. And nevahhhh come back. I mean it."

With that, she slammed the apartment door in my face.

I walked away, smiling at her drama, as she howled with crazy-lady laughter on the other side of the door.

12

MARLON

KEALY STRODE INTO THE CROWDED BRUNCH SPOT LIKE SHE
owned the place. It was one of the things I liked about her.
She was just naturally self-possessed—not cocky or full of
herself like so many in the fashion world, but charmingly
down to earth and unassuming.

Not to mention, gorgeous.

I caught her eye and waved. She broke out in a big smile
as she wove between the closely packed tables to get to me.

"Oh, my god, am I late? I'm sorry, I must be late," she
said breathlessly. She untangled herself from her cross-
body bag and removed her hoodie to reveal a white T-shirt
that showed off her lovely shape.

I couldn't help but laugh. I reached for her hand.
"You're fine, Kealy, really. I got here early to get a table."

Surprise crossed her face, followed by appreciation. "Thank you, that was really nice."

"Well, you had to leave so abruptly last night, I figured it was the least I could do to continue showing you a good time."

"Ugh. I'm so sorry about my roommate. She said she'd send you a replacement plant."

"Totally not necessary, and don't worry about it. Bloody Mary?" I asked.

"Yes, please," she said, glancing through the menu.

Damn, she was cute with that blunt cut blonde hair. It gave her a kind of edgy look that so many New York women were after but couldn't quite pull off. But on her, it was perfection. And then there were those green eyes…

"Marlon? Marlon, are you okay?" she asked.

Shit. "Yeah, I'm sorry. I was just mesmerized by your eyes." No sense in beating around the bush.

"Oh. Thanks," she said, a pink tinge washing over her face.

She was a blusher. Yowsa, that got me.

The waiter took our orders and rushed away. One of the things I loved about the Uptown was that they brought your food *fast.*

Not five minutes later I was watching Kealy dig into her eggs benedict.

"So, Rand tells me you've had some challenges at work lately," I said.

Her head snapped up, and she stopped chewing.

"Hey, we guys are buddies, and we all want to learn a bit

more about you. Anyway, didn't mean to throw you off guard," I said.

She was silent for a moment and then nodded slowly. "Yeah. A guy I work with pirated some of my work. In fact, he was at your party. I think you know him. Muse?"

"The little guy who wears the bowties?"

She nodded. "Marlon, are you guys friends with him?"

"Not really. I mean, we know him from the shows. That model brought him, the really bitchy one who's always popping pills."

"Oh yeah, I spotted her across the room."

"Well, I'm not sure how *she* got invited, but you know how parties are. The word gets out...people show up," I said.

"They destroy your plants...all in a day's party." She smiled guiltily.

Seriously, I could give a shit about that stupid tree her roommate trampled all over. Someone had given me that plant when I'd moved in. In fact, every plant I had was given to me. It never would have occurred to me to buy a single houseplant. Except maybe a cactus. I liked those, and they seemed hard to kill.

"So, what are you going to do about work? I mean, it sounds like your boss didn't really support you," I said.

I knew what it was like to not be supported. Unfortunately.

She dabbed her mouth with her napkin. "You know what I want to do? Start my own men's wear collection."

She shrugged and leaned closer. "It's really a dream at this point, so I'm keeping it kind of quiet."

I raised my hand like a Boy Scout. "Promise. Won't tell a soul."

She was gorgeous *and* had drive. That was a package I liked.

"What's your timeframe for kicking things off?" Christ, I sounded like the kind of corporate creep I'd spent my life trying to avoid.

She pursed her lips for a moment. "I don't know. I suppose it's a pipe dream. It takes a lot of money to launch a label."

"Well, I'd like to see some of your work. I mean, I guess I have seen it. Shit, I've worn it at the shows. Hey, those weird trousers were your design, weren't they?"

Oops. Had I just stuck my foot in my mouth? Well, this would be the perfect way to see if she had a sense of humor.

"Yeah, yeah. Cross told me they weren't a hit with you guys. But the fashion press loved them," she said.

"Well, there you go. If they're a bellwether for what will sell, I say go for it. What do I know? I just wear the stuff." I gestured toward myself. "As you can see, in the off hours, I am a jeans and T-shirt kind of guy."

She laughed again. "That's cool. There will never been anything that *everyone* loves. It's impossible."

Whew. Skated through that one.

She tilted her head and looked at me. "What about you? I mean, what's your story?"

I leaned back in my chair. "Oh, right. My story. Well, I dropped out of college and have been on my parents' shit list ever since."

"Why'd you drop out?"

I shrugged. "I wanted to travel. See the world. That sort of thing. I mean, I'll go back to college one day. I just don't want to right now."

"Well, why were your parents so opposed to that? I mean, it sounds pretty reasonable," she said.

"My dad wanted me in the family business. He's pretty powerful and used to getting his way. He owns one of the NFL teams and wanted me to work with him."

Her eyes bugged out of her head. I was used to that. It happened every time I told someone what my dad did. It was why I didn't talk about it. But if I wanted to know Kealy, I had to let her know me.

"Your dad owns a football team?" she said slowly.

"Yup. Sure does."

She nodded, a chunk of her blonde hair falling across her eye.

Oh, what the hell.

I reached out and tucked it behind her ear. And don't you know, just as I did, she leaned into my hand.

Christ, I was dying to kiss her. But there'd be time for that.

"It's just not really my thing, though, working with my dad. You know what I mean?" I asked.

"What do you want to do, if not work for a sports team?"

If I only knew.

"At some point, I'd like to do something entrepreneurial. Start something of my own rather than take the safe route and follow Dad. Until then, modeling is good. It pays the bills, and the hours aren't too bad."

"So is that how you have such an amazing apartment? Because your family is well-off?" she asked.

I knew she'd put two and two together. You didn't have a home like mine in Manhattan without help from someone.

"Yeah. When my grandmother died, she left me money. I was fortunate enough to snag that place in Soho."

I paid the bill, and we got up to leave, forced to weave back around the tight tables that were just as packed as when we arrived. The thing about weekend brunch in New York was that it never seemed to end. It started in the morning and went straight through 'til dinner. And a restaurant like Uptown was always mobbed.

Out in the sunshine, I took a chance and draped an arm around Kealy's shoulder. She pressed into me as we walked, which was a damn good sign.

"So, my green-eyed friend," I said, stopping, "I'm quite impressed with you."

She looked down shyly, but quickly back up at me with her usual confidence. "Really? And why would that be, my brown-eyed friend?" she asked.

"You have enough self-respect to not let a set-back put you out of business. You've got a plan B and have thought it out. You're kind, as witnessed in the way you took care of your drunk friend. And you're fucking hot."

I didn't really need to add that last piece, but it kind of slipped out.

I bent to kiss her, and she was delicious and lovely, just like I knew she'd be. Her lips welcomed mine with a pliant response, and when they parted slightly, well, my pulse sped up double time. I was hungry—no, starving—for the other things I wanted to do with her, but I knew to take my time.

I had plenty of time.

13

KEALY

I COULDN'T BE FRIENDS WITH PEOPLE WHO WOULDN'T RIDE the subway.

It was rigid and judgmental of me to think that way—all things I normally tried really hard not to be—but New York's subway was the great equalizer, and if someone felt they were above riding it, well, then they shouldn't hang out with me.

And what was Marlon's take on it?

Let's just say the guy did not let me down. In fact, it was his idea to grab the subway after brunch. His suggestion was music to my ears.

"Why are you smiling so brightly?" he asked as we descended the subway steps. Holding hands.

We hustled along. There was no strolling when it came to public transit. If you were going to take it, then you had to commit to moving your ass. On the way to a stuffy platform that smelled liked a homeless person's pee, you had to move like you were being chased by a wild animal.

It made no sense, I know. A lot of things about New York made no sense. A lot of things about life, and especially *my* life, made no sense.

Like why, after years of being bounced around in the foster system, did I suddenly fall into the warm embrace of a family like Marina's that came to love, support, and believe in me?

Talk about extremes. I wouldn't have minded if the ups and downs had been a little less mountainous, a little less dramatic. But that's not the way life had been for me.

"I really like the subway. In fact, I kind of love it," I told him.

I looked up at him. Actually, looked *way* up at him, that's how tall he was. His brown skin glistened with a thin layer of perspiration from walking, and it didn't help that the platform had zero air circulation. That is, until a train roared into the station whipping the muggy overheated air into a wave that smacked you across the face. It would invade your nostrils as deeply as any smell could, leaving you with the taste of it on your tongue and the ooze of it trickling into your pores. Blech.

But like I said, I loved it. There were so many things about New York that were a pain in the ass, that the one thing that was relatively easy and cheap got my utmost respect.

I leaned against one of the vertical beams on the

subway platform that held a sign saying *72nd Street*, and Marlon moved closer until I was pretty much sandwiched between him and it. He leaned on the beam by placing a hand above my head.

"I can't say I've ever heard anyone say they loved the subway," he said quietly, moving closer and closer

"Really? Well, everyone else is crazy. I'm the normal one," I said.

And even though we were in my adored dirty, stinky subway, I felt like I was on top of the world at that moment. Winning the lottery could not have made me feel better than having this gorgeous man hovering over me, looking at me like I was awesome. I hadn't felt special many times in my life and certainly hadn't since Muse had screwed me over and Forest ignored my appeals. But for that moment in time, I did.

"Thank you," I said quietly.

"For what?"

"Oh, everything. Brunch, inviting me to your party, taking the subway. Looking at me like that."

He moved a little closer, and I could feel his warm breath. Ten trains could have gone by and I would not have noticed.

"How am I looking at you, Kealy?" he asked.

Goddamn, he was hot.

"Like you want to kiss me. Really badly," I said.

Booyah.

Thank god I was leaning against something.

"Well, that's funny. Because I do want to kiss you badly.

But I'm not surprised you figured it out. You're a smart girl." He breathed the words onto my lips, and when he was done speaking, overwhelmed me with a sweet kiss I found myself wishing would never end. His lips were soft and gentle, the perfect contrast to his huge hand that hooked a couple fingers under my chin.

My breath started to come in short gasps, and if I wasn't careful, I knew I'd be tearing my clothes off right there on the subway platform. And his too.

"Mmmm," he murmured. "Sweet girl."

He pulled back, took my hand, and led me onto the train that had just pulled into the station.

MARLON DROPPED me off in front of my building before he got back on the subway to continue home. I floated up to my apartment, captivated by…well, everything.

"Keal? That you?" Fantine called from the sofa.

"Nope. It's a burglar."

"Hey, that's not funny," she said.

"Okay, then. Yes, it's me."

She clicked off her movie, sat up, and crossed her arms.

"Geez. Is something wrong?" I asked. You never knew with her whether she was mad about something or just being dramatic.

"Spill it. I want to hear everything. And is he mad at me about the plant?"

I took a deep breath. "Well, first, he could not care less about the plant. Said he didn't even really like it anyway."

She nodded, relieved she didn't have to spend money on something other than clothes or shoes.

"And…?" God, she was demanding.

"He's awesome. I freaking love his bald head. And he has the longest, curliest eyelashes, but strong hands, and god, could he kiss."

"Nice," she said, drawing out the word. "Ya kissed him. That's awesome."

A heat washed over my face. Was I blushing in front of Fantine? What the hell was I embarrassed about? Or was it just excitement?

Satisfied that I'd gotten a kiss out of the date, Fantine had happily returned to flipping the TV channels, looking for something more interesting than me. Which wasn't saying much.

So, I forged ahead. I'd have her full and undivided attention momentarily.

Three…two…one…

"I talked to Marlon a bit about the sharing thing."

She didn't even look away from the TV.

"Yeah? What about it?"

When I didn't continue, she stopped flipping and placed the remote on the coffee table in front of her.

"How does it work?"

That was a good question.

"Like they all date one woman at the same time. Marlon said it was hot as hell."

"Wow. Just wow. Better than a threesome. A five-some! You'll have a harem of good-looking men. I mean, shit, they're male models. You just hit the man jackpot."

I'd hit on something. Wasn't sure what, though.

AFTER SPENDING the rest of the weekend sacked on the couch with Fantine, watching one Netflix show after the other while I sketched new designs, I was raring to go to work Monday morning. I hadn't felt that way in a while. Maybe I was getting my mojo back?

But before I did, I pulled out my sewing machine and set it up in place of the two-person kitchenette table we only ever used as a dumping ground. I ran my fingers over my prized possession; a used Swiss model I'd scraped together the money to buy. I loved it with every inch of my being. Because we had a couple industrial machines at the office, I normally used those when I needed to sew something quickly. But what I was planning to work on now had to be done in the privacy of my own home.

We always had extra, unused fabric at the studio left over from whatever the sample sewers were working on. We ended up with huge quantities of fabric sometimes, which we would donate to the area fashion schools, unless someone in the office wanted it. In fact, that was pretty much how I ended up working for Forest—I loved his men's wear fabrics and asked for an internship. One thing led to another and *boom*, I was in. Forest gave me a chance, and even though I was disappointed in him because of recent developments, I still had a soft spot for him.

So my plan was to be completely silent about my at-home projects and draw no notice to myself with the fabrics I was allowed to take home. I mean, if someone were to ask, I could always fib and say I was working on something for a friend—which was kind of true because I always made my friends test my designs. But I was keeping my cards close to the vest from now on.

The old confidence was seeping back, thank god. Not that I'd had doubts about my design abilities, no. It was more like, *was I back to getting shit on by life or was all that in the past?* That was haunting the hell out of me. But I'd taken that unfortunate line of thinking and squashed it like an ugly bug in the middle of the living room floor. *Hell, no.* I wouldn't go back to where I'd started. I just wouldn't. Kid in the foster system, bounced from one house to another, not really wanted by anyone, told I'd not amount to anything. Well, that might have been a person I once knew.

But it was one I didn't know any more.

14

SHANE

It was finally my turn to spend some time with the lovely Kealy, and I was damn happy about it. In fact, I didn't even mind that my kids' basketball team had just been trounced by the community center across town.

Where I'd grown up in Ireland, there wasn't much for kids to do with their free time. No clubs or organized sports, not for miles. So, I'd always been the one to pull together enough boys—and girls if they wanted to join— for a football game or two. When I came to the States, to say I was surprised to find that football—actually, soccer— was only moderately popular was an understatement. So, I joined a basketball league because that's what a lot of American guys seemed to like.

Boy, did I suck when I first started playing. But after much ridicule and humiliation, not to mention twisted ankles and elbows to the face, I got the hang of basketball well enough to coach kids in my spare time.

That day's game had not gone as planned, but I wasn't going to get down about the loss. You win some and lose some, and besides, these were just ten-year-old kids. I sent them home with their parents after the game and hopped into the locker room shower. I didn't mind being stinky around the guys—Rand, Marlon, and Cross—and in fact, I loved to torture them with my sweaty stench, but I wasn't about to foist that on our Kealy. It was hard to date a woman who couldn't wait to get away from you.

Not fifteen minutes later, I was clean and smelling as sweet as I ever would. My cell beeped, letting me know Kealy was close by, and I went out in front of the center to meet her.

And boy, was I glad I did. I had the immense pleasure of admiring her confident and unassuming stroll as she walked down the street, checking out the neighborhood. She moved with purpose, like everyone in New York learned to do, but she was also taking in her surroundings, which were new to her. No one came to this neighborhood unless they lived here, or had an express reason to be here, like I did for my volunteering. It just wasn't where you went for a stroll.

I knew that all too well.

"Shane!" she called, unaware I'd been watching her, which was just as well. Not many women I knew liked feeling stalked.

"Well, hello, beautiful," I said, leaning in to kiss her cheek. "Thank you for coming all the way here."

"My pleasure," she said, looking around the scruffy neighborhood. "It's always nice to see a new part of the city."

She was completed unfazed by the run-down houses and graffiti. There was more to this woman than met the eye, and I looked forward to learning what made her tick.

I nodded, looking around. "Ya know, the most wonderful people live here. They don't have much, but they're tight with their families and look out for their neighbors. 'Course the neighborhood does have its downsides, but I prefer to focus on the positive."

"So, you think you can teach me to shoot hoops?" she asked with a grin.

"Let's go find out," I said, holding the door for her.

We headed straight for the gym, a grand old room, musty and a little tired with a warped floor, but not without its charms. Old-school skylights helped brightened the place, and stained glass artwork spanned the transom spaces over the broad auditorium doors.

"Love this!" Kealy said, twirling three-hundred-sixty-degrees.

"Let's go up in the bleachers and take in all in." I extended my hand, which she took without hesitation.

I liked that.

"Just think of all the people who've come through this room, and how many sports have been coached, and how many games have been played," she said wistfully.

I turned to look at her when we were settled into the bleachers' top row.

"Sounds like you have a place like this in your past," I said.

She looked at her hands for a moment. "I suppose. I went to a bunch of schools, growing up."

"A lot of people would not have been comfortable in this neighborhood, but I noticed you were pretty unfazed," I said.

She nodded slowly. "Yeah, a lot of my youth was in neighborhoods just like this. I guess you could say I'm pretty comfortable in places like this. For a long time, it was all I knew."

"No kidding. Tell me more." After several deafening basketball games earlier in the day, the gym was eerily quiet, like a sleeping giant. I loved it when it was crazy, and I loved it when it was quiet.

"I grew up in foster care and was bounced around a lot. I may have gone to a school with a gym like this, but they've all run together in my memory over the years."

"I guess you're one of the foster system's success stories," I said.

She smiled, and I could have sworn, in spite of that, something sad washed over her face. "Not sure I would say that. But I did get a lucky break. Everyone should get at least one lucky break in life. 'Course some people get lots of them, and some people don't get a damn one."

"Isn't that the truth? What was yours?" I asked.

"I got a nanny job with a family here, and they took a liking to me. Helped me get into college and even paid for part of it. I'd never had anyone in my life like that."

"Wow. You keep up with them?"

"Oh, my god, yes. Marina—the mom—is like a big sister to me. And a fairy godmother. And a mentor. She always has my back. In fact, when I was recently having some issues at work, she immediately took me to lunch and gave me the best pep-talk ever. I'd be nowhere without those people."

I looked at the beautiful Kealy. I'd been right. She did have a story. And I loved a woman with a story. Silly, shallow girls, step aside.

And damn if I couldn't stop staring into those green eyes.

I raked a hand through my hair. "You know, speaking of your work, I overheard something strange at the party at Marlon's last week, and I think it might have to do with you."

She crinkled her nose. "Me? What did you hear, Shane?"

"Well, I was in the kitchen making myself a drink—I'm sure you remember how crowded that party was—and I overheard a guy bragging about pulling one over on his boss."

Shit. Should I have continued? She didn't need anything to add to her work miseries. But on the other hand, if my eavesdropping could help her, I didn't want to hold back.

"So, the guy was saying that for Forest's latest collection, he'd gotten credit for a lot of the work done by the rest of the team. He thought it was funny and was laughing about it."

My poor girl paled, as if someone had just punched her in the gut, and I guessed the info I shared had done just that. She pressed her lips together in a thin line, and looked out over the auditorium from our high perch. I could see her thought process and knew she had the character to resist the victim claim and move into fighter mode.

"Was the guy wearing a bowtie?" she asked very quietly.

Shit. She knew exactly who I was talking about. I nodded and took her hand.

"I'm sorry to upset you," I said.

She shook her head. "No. Thank you for telling me. I already knew it had happened but was not aware he thought it was amusing. Something about that is even more maddening than my designs being ripped off. That he has so little respect not only for me, but also our boss, who is a good guy."

She was pissed, and that was good. She'd take action, and I could see her kicking ass as soon as she figured out how to deal with the situation. She wasn't going to take this, or any other kind of bullshit, lying down. My kind of girl.

"Did he say anything else, that you heard?" she asked, looking at me with watery eyes.

"Just that he thought his actions would eventually pay off, whatever that meant. Look, I'm sorry I've upset you—"

She held her hand up in a *stop* motion. "No. This is

good. I needed to hear this. I thought that guy was my friend and he screwed me over."

I reached to tuck some hair behind her ear. God, I wanted to kiss her, make her feel better. She hadn't asked for much out of life, and wasn't moving through it like an entitled jerk, unlike so many other people I knew.

"Kealy, you'll come out of this on top. Don't ask me how I know this, but I just do."

"Thanks, Shane. You're so great. All you guys are." Her head snapped in my direction. She was clearly wondering if she'd just said something she shouldn't have.

With all that she had going on, the last thing she needed to be worrying about was us guys.

"Hey. Let me set something straight. We guys all like you. We hide nothing from each other. If you spend time with one of us, and then another the next day, that's awesome. That's what we want, as long as it's what you want."

"I just don't know about this business of dating multiple men, particularly who are friends. It just seems…weird."

I wanted to reassure her, but she was smart and needed time. She had to see for herself that it would work and that we could all make her happy. But she wouldn't come to know that overnight.

"Hey, no pressure. Whatever you feel is right is what I— and the other guys—want for you. You don't have to be embarrassed or apologize for spending time with any of us. Ever," I added.

She brushed a hand over my knee and gave me a sly

little smile that made my pulse race. If we didn't get down on the basketball court and practice shooting some hoops, I wasn't sure I'd be able to resist taking her behind the bleachers and kissing her properly, like she deserved.

15

KEALY

I just barely avoided a broken nose.

That would have sucked. Seriously.

Shane, with all the patience I expected of a kids' coach, was trying to help me make a basket. I held the ball above my head in the position he'd shown me. He stood behind me and with his hands over mine, guided me as I chucked the ball forward and up.

When it hit the rim of the basket, I was delighted. But when it ricocheted directly back toward my face, I ducked just in time.

Maybe basketball dates weren't for me.

But hey, I was game for anything, so with several more tries, while remaining alert to potential nose-breakers, I actually got one in the basket. Well, it's kind of overstating it to say *I* got it in the basket. At least fifty percent of the effort came from Shane. Maybe more.

But that didn't mean I didn't love having his arms around me. I played it cool, but I could totally tell he was smelling my hair when he spent so much time trying to get me to hold the ball just right. I had to admit, I messed up just a little to keep his arms around me.

I could be sneaky that way.

"Now, I'm gonna teach you how to steal the ball," he said.

I was sure I'd shine at that, just like I'd shone at dunking baskets. Or dunking the ball. Or whatever the saying was.

No, I was not much of a sports fan. But when a gorgeous red head with a slightly crooked nose and heavy Irish accent came along as a bonus, I could suffer through most any athletic effort. Especially when it included strong arms around me.

So he was bouncing the ball around the gym, expecting me to run after him and somehow swipe it from his hands, which were moving at the speed of light. I think we both knew I wouldn't be stealing much of anything, unless it was a kiss.

Speaking of which. Now that I wanted to kiss him, he was running away from me. Story of my life.

So, I feigned out of breath-ness. Doubled over, holding my side.

"I think I might have a bit of a cramp," I lied.

"Oh, shit," he said, dropping the ball. "Let me get you some water."

That was cool. I'd take some water. But I had to remember I had a side cramp. That was the problem with lying. If you weren't used to it—which I wasn't—you got all confused and messed up your story.

But I had a feeling he'd forgive me if I said something contradictory.

I fake-limped over to the bleachers, doubled over and holding my side, and wondered if I should be moaning to come off as more authentic. If I'd had the time, I might have Googled *side stitch*, but he was back too fast with my cool water.

I gulped down what he'd brought me and took a big inhale.

"I think it's going away. Thank you for the water," I said, looking up at him.

How long was I supposed to be incapacitated by pain? Dammit, I didn't know. That was why people shouldn't lie. Or it's why I shouldn't lie. I sucked at it.

Oh, fuck it.

I popped up and placed a hand on either side of his rugged face. He didn't have the usual model looks, aside from his height, but when you put all the pieces of him together, you ended up with something very appealing.

Very.

And he seemed to like that I'd recovered so quickly because in an instant, his lips were on mine.

Good lord, he smelled great—a combo of spicy, clean soap mixed with the lightest bit of basketball perspiration. It was so goddamn *manly*. And he tasted like mint, maybe from toothpaste or mouthwash, I wasn't sure. But my head grew light, and if I didn't get something to lean against soon, I might be toppling over. And not from a side cramp.

He pulled back from our kiss to look at me. "You're fucking beautiful, you know that?"

I wasn't sure I'd ever gotten a compliment quite like that, which was so visceral and unplanned and goddamn *sincere*. I wanted to melt into his arms. He believed in me, was handsome, and had three other gorgeous friends.

Oh, shit. Did I just say that?

I couldn't date four guys, whether they were friends or not.

But I'd worry about that later.

I sank my lips into his soft mouth and inhaled enough of him to know I wanted more. But we were in the damn community center. There was no one around, as far as I could tell, but I didn't want to get down and dirty in freaking public.

Or did I?

"Hey, is there someplace a bit more private that we could go?" I was trying to be sultry, but my heated, red face gave me away.

Of course, Shane was too polite to notice, or even mention, my blushing problem.

"I know where we can go. C'mon," he said, pulling me by the hand.

I grabbed my bag off the bench and ran after him in my high-top Chucks, which I'd worn just for our workout. I wanted to look the part. I did work in fashion, after all.

He led me to a men's locker room, which I fully expected to be filthy and polluted with foul smells. But either no one ever used it, or the cleaning crew had recently been there, because it was cleaner than my own house.

Before letting the door swing closed behind us, I looked around to check for other people.

"Are you sure this is okay? I mean, where is everyone? Isn't this a community center?"

"Yeah, but staff are here mostly when there are sports or classes going on. In the evening, if nothing's on the calendar, everyone goes home."

Oh. Well, then.

The locker room was the old-fashioned kind with oak lockers and benches, and a green tiled floor. In a far corner was a stack of white towels and next to it, a basket for dirty ones. As I followed Shane, I passed an old-school communal shower room, a bathroom with urinals, and a windowed room with all kinds of sports equipment.

Shane sat on one of the narrow benches running between a short row of lockers and pulled me onto him, forcing me to straddle his legs as I faced him. His mouth crashed into me with the fury of a starving man, and he gripped my hair so hard, the sting took my breath.

I ran my hands over his mountainous shoulders and down the faded old T-shirt obscuring his hard chest. My hands were trembling, and as he pulled me toward him and I ground against his growing erection, there was a flood of wet warmth in my panties.

Down, girl.

"Mmmm," he murmured. "You smell so nice, and your lips taste even better," he crooned.

And of course, I kissed him harder.

His hands wandered over the front of my blouse and began to pick at the buttons until I felt cool air on my chest. In moments, he'd pushed up my bra and began to nibble and suck my screaming nipples.

Good lord. I was only just getting to know this guy, and yet I was comfortable enough to mess around with him in the locker room of a community center. Couldn't say I'd ever done that.

His growing erection pressed against me where I was straddling him and I couldn't help but grind back. Was he going to think I was kinky?

But how could he? I mean, he and his friends were the ones who freaking *shared* women. If that wasn't kinky, I didn't know what was.

Shane stood and spun me in such a quick movement I didn't realize what was happening until I was on my back on the narrow locker room bench. His hands flew to my jeans as he worked my belt and zipper, while his gaze remained locked with mine, as if to check in and make sure I was on board. But I was so freaking turned on he could have done anything to me and I would have let him. So I gave him a small smile while my hands played with my sensitive tits.

He got my jeans down to my knees and paused only to yank off my Chucks. When one leg was free of my pants, he spread my legs as wide as they would possibly go. Positioning himself between them, he paused and stared.

"Beautiful pussy." He ran a finger through my slit, and it came out so wet, I was a teeny bit embarrassed. But when he put it in his mouth and closed his eyes to savor my tang, any inhibitions I had flew out the door. I didn't know what changed. But something had.

He lunged forward, initially startling me, until his tongue circled my clit with the most exquisite skillfulness. I arched to push myself into him and lolled my head back and forth on the hard bench, which was no longer hard nor uncomfortable. It was as if every nerve ending in my body centered between my legs and the rest of me had just gone numb. There was no feeling anywhere but where Shane touched me.

And boy, was he touching me. His thumb ventured inside me just an inch while he licked and sucked me like a starving man. He held one of my thighs with his other hand in a bruising grip that I knew would leave marks later.

"God...oh, god..." I cried as I came, racked with powerful spasms that left me shuddering violently.

I clawed at his hair for purchase and pulled him closer to my soaked pussy while I lost myself in a crazy, furious rut. I couldn't have let him go if I'd even wanted to, that's how strongly he possessed me.

He pulled his head free of my hands, and circling my clit, rubbed me into another explosive orgasm.

As I came down, he dragged me to sitting and pressed

his lips against mine, sharing my taste. I collapsed in his arms, completely spent. I don't know how long it took, but he helped me get dressed and we later wandered out into the fresh night air. He hailed the first cab he saw. I was too out of it to insist on the subway.

We'd have to cover that later.

16

CROSS

"She's a lovely lass, my friend," Shane said, lifting a beer bottle to his lips.

"Awesome. I'm seeing her this weekend. I feel like I might be ready to get out there again after losing Mary."

Shane nodded. "Sure, buddy. It's been a long journey."

Joey shifted in my arms. He'd fallen asleep there after dinner, and I didn't want to wake him. His nanny was usually around to help me put him to bed, but she had had a family thing that night. Which was fine with me. And Shane was always happy to come over for free beer and to see my little guy who called him *Shay*. A two-year-old was going to do what a two-year-old did, and that included talking like one.

When I was finally convinced my little man was down for the count, I carefully carried him to his crib. Shane followed me, happy to participate in the bedtime ritual since he'd come from a family of seven kids. He'd have his own someday and would be an awesome dad.

"How was your game the other day?" I asked when we'd settled back in my living room.

"Ah, the little ones are terrible, but they are so darn funny. And sweet. You should see them."

"I'd love to come sometime." Actually, I wished I had time for a volunteer activity like Shane's. But with the kid, and working as much as I could…

"I had Kealy down at the Community Center. Showed her some basketball moves…and other things." He looked down at his hands and smiled.

We guys were close, but we didn't kiss and tell. At least, not much.

"I like her, Cross, I do. We were having so much fun, we lost track of time. I got us the hell out of there before it got too late."

"Still don't feel safe down there, do you?" I asked.

His hand absentmindedly wandered up to his chest, and he shrugged. "I hate to say it because I love my volunteering, but ever since I was jumped, I don't stay in the neighborhood much past dark."

"You all healed up where they got you?" I asked.

He rubbed the spot where he'd been stabbed during the mugging. Poor guy, it clearly still haunted him. "Well, you've seen the scar. Can't model topless anymore," he said with a smirk.

"Unless they want someone really badass looking."

"Yeah, I was already badass looking enough without a huge scar on my chest."

I shook my head. "Hey. Everyone loves a badass Irishman."

"Well, I hope the lovely Kealy loves—or at least likes—this badass Irishman. Because I sure have taken a liking to her."

THE WEEK CRAWLED by in spite of my non-stop schedule of running from modeling gig to Joey, and back. It was busy season for photo shoots, and my agent had me lined up for every catalogue and print ad she could get me in. I was obsessive about putting a chunk of money aside for Joey, and this allowed me the comfort of doing that. It was the least I could do—this little guy had already lost his mom, a beautiful, amazing woman whom I'd miss until my dying days. As long as I could do the jobs with minimal time away from my kid, it was all good. And his nanny loved him almost as much as I did.

So every spare moment when wasn't busy, I found my thoughts wandering to Kealy. I'd not been interested in anyone in a long time, but something about her plucky ambition and hot as hell good looks kept her in the forefront of my mind. And it was perfect that the other guys felt the same way. Something about it felt alive, and I hadn't dated a women along with the other guys since long before I'd gotten married.

I headed out to meet her Saturday afternoon, as soon as the nanny arrived to look after Joey. We'd decided to keep things mellow with a long stroll around the city, and then a simple dinner at her favorite Italian joint. She'd seemed pretty psyched about our getting together, so I was excited to see if the chemistry would be there.

"Hey," I said when I found her at our meeting place—a bench in Washington Square park.

She looked up from her book and smiled. Fuck, if she wasn't gorgeous. Her messy blonde hair and cross-body bag lent a tomboyish air to her, but her perfect hourglass proportions and graceful movement were about as feminine as a woman could get. It was the perfect combination.

And I liked unique women. My wife had been one.

Kealy popped up from her seat, tucking her book into her bag.

"Great to see you." She threw her arms around me in a warm, friendly embrace. I took a deep inhale, smelling plain soap and a slight bit of rose perfume. We started strolling.

I loved the city, and never tired of walking everywhere I could, usually dragging Joey along with me in his stroller or on my shoulders. I took it as a good sign that Kealy liked walking, too.

"They've really cleaned up this area," I said as we headed toward the Lower East Side.

"Yeah? I don't know this part of town very well. It's cool. This is where a lot of immigrants started out when they first came to the United States, right?"

"Exactly. People came here from all over Europe, trying to make it in the new world."

We turned down a little alley that was probably a rough and tumble tenement row back in the day. But now, with gentrification, it was about as charming as it could be with pots of geraniums hanging from every windowsill and a pretty bench in front of each house.

"Funny how this area is so desirable now, when it was probably full of dirt poor people without plumbing or proper heat in the winter," Kealy said.

I loved that she wasn't ignorant of the city's history.

"How'd you get into modeling, Cross?" she asked.

"Oh, I started a long time ago, geez, when I was in high school. My mom would drive me around to these go-sees. I hated it. Just wanted to be with my friends. But the money I made really helped my family, so I stuck with it. And years later, here I am, still doing it."

"Do you like it?" she asked.

"You know, when I was younger, and it was all about partying and meeting girls, it was tons of fun. Opened lots of doors. But when I met Joey's mom and fell in love, it became a job. Which wasn't a bad thing, but I was doing it to support my family."

I took her hand and led her to a bright green bench outside what looked to be a very expensive, restored brick building. It was so funny that what was probably once a shithole was now something worth millions of dollars.

"How'd you end up in fashion?" I asked.

Her face lit up. "Well, I'd always loved to sketch

garments and figure out how to sew them. And when I was a nanny for the Benson's, who turned out to be the family I'd never had before, Marina—the mom—saw my sketches and sewing and got me into fashion school. I got an internship with Forest, and here I am today."

"You like it there?" I asked.

I had a feeling I knew what answer was coming, but I wanted to hear it from her.

She looked down at her hands. "Until recently, I loved it."

"I heard a blowhard little asshole at Marlon's party bragging about ripping you off. I wanted to say something to him, but Shane convinced me it was your battle to fight. So maybe we could all fight it together?"

"What do you mean?"

I swiveled on the bench to face her, and to be honest, get a better look at those glittery eyes of hers. "We—Rand, Marlon, Shane, and I—might be able to help you. I've already heard you are interested in starting a collection of your own."

An expensively dressed couple with multiple shopping bags clicked down the alley toward their rowhouse. Kealy watched them walk by, and then looked at me.

"What do you mean? How can you help?" she asked, confusion troubling her pretty face.

"Well, that's one of the things I wanted to talk to you about today. What do you say we head to dinner, and discuss it there?" I asked, standing.

I reached for her hand to help her up and kept ahold of

if after she'd risen to her feet. She looked at our clasped hands, and then at me, smiling lightly. She closed her eyes.

The perfect invitation.

I lowered my lips to hers and knew life was about to change.

17

KEALY

"Can I get you anything else?" the waiter asked as he dropped off our tiramisu.

Cross and I shook our heads as we grabbed our spoons and lunged for the dessert in front of us.

I was already stuffed to the gills from antipasti and chicken *picatta*, but there was no way I was going to pass on the city's best tiramisu. Year after year, the little Italian joint on my corner was voted the best in New York magazine, and I could vouch for its accuracy.

I closed my eyes. "Oh, my god, this is unreal. I'll never get tired of it." I heard the dessert plate sliding across the table *away from me*, so I quickly opened my eyes.

"Hey! What are you doing?" I asked, reaching for the bowl that Cross was trying to hijack.

"C'mon. You live here. You can get this stuff anytime. I

might never be back here," he said, trying not to laugh. "Can't you have some pity on me?"

"Okay. I'll tell ya right now, you do not want to get between this girl and her dessert."

Although the thought of wrestling him didn't sound half bad. He was so goddamn good-looking with his messy man-bun and facial scruff. I could just imagine him pinning my arms above my head to the ground so I couldn't move...

Relax, would ya?

"So, Cross. I hope you don't mind, but I wanted to ask what happened to Joey's mom." I set down my spoon and leaned forward with attention.

In spite of his beautiful smile, a sadness washed across his face that made my heart break a little. I'd had my share of ups and downs, but I'd never lost someone I was in love with. What would that even be like? And how would you live through it?

He put his spoon down, too, and leaned onto the table.

"Mary. She had a bad flu, and a couple weeks later, was gone. The whole thing was unbelievable. Joey was just a baby. He was still nursing, for Christ's sake," he said, looking down at his white-knuckled hands.

I reached across the table and placed my fingers over his.

"Oh, my god. I'm so sorry." My eyes filled with tears.

He nodded slowly. "Thank you. Yeah, it's been quite a time. That's why I work so much. I want to make sure Joey is always looked after, in case something were to happen to me."

"I don't blame you. I'd do the same."

He waved the waiter down for the check, but I shoved my credit card in the man's hand before Cross could.

He looked at me exasperated, but I just shrugged and smiled. I had a damn job and could pay once in a while.

WITHOUT SAYING A WORD, I held the crook of Cross's elbow and we headed straight for my apartment. I knew Fantine would be home, so I'd sneaked in a little text to warn her before we left the restaurant. Actually, I didn't mind at all that she was home—god knew I'd listened her get down with a few guys before—but I didn't want her chewing our ear off so long that Cross would have to head out to send his baby-sitter home before I could have some fun with him.

And true to her word, when we walked into the apartment, she hollered *hi* from her bedroom and softly shut the door.

I owed her for that.

"Hey, cute apartment," Cross said, doing a three-sixty to take in the miniscule place. I suspected he only made a full circle to make me feel better for living in such small digs. Honestly, you could see pretty much the entire place from the front doorway. You barely had to turn your head.

"Wow. Fancy sewing machine," he said, looking at my baby.

The man knew his way into a girl's heart. At least, a sewing girl's heart.

"This machine has carried me through thick and thin and is about to be tested with carrying me to the next phase of my life."

"Whoa. That's a lot of pressure to put on a small machine," he said, smiling.

He had a point. And that damn smile got my heart pounding. But I wasn't going to let on. At least, not yet.

"Well, maybe I have too many eggs in one basket, but we got big plans, my sewing machine and me." I put some tea on and led him to the sofa that was still warm from Fantine's little behind.

"And how are you going to approach these big plans?" he asked.

"I've been stockpiling leftover fabric that would usually go to the design schools," I said, pointing to the piles in the corner of the living room. Thank god Fantine didn't mind my spreading out in our little apartment.

Another thing I owed her for.

"I've been staying late at work making patterns for my new designs. As soon as they're done, I'll start sewing samples."

"Cool. That's actually what I wanted to talk to you about tonight."

"Yeah. What did you mean by you and the guys 'supporting me?'" I asked.

"Well, we know you're talented, and with the connections we have in the industry, we think we could help you make a go of it. Hell, at the very least, we could model the collection for you."

Holy shit. Life *was* turning in a new direction. A fucking *great* direction.

My eyes filled with tears once again, but not because of sadness this time. "Oh, my god. Thank you, Cross. Thank you for believing in me." I ran my fingers through the scruffy beard on his chin.

He gently pushed me back onto the sofa until I was lying down, and balanced above me on one elbow. His mouth met mine as I wrapped my legs around him.

He was beautiful and perfect, his breath quickening as I pressed my hips into his growing erection. I wanted to touch him there, actually everywhere, but I restrained myself.

I tipped my head back to expose my neck, and his soft lips brushed over my skin in a delicious indulgence. It didn't matter that I was in a crappy little apartment with my roommate just feet away and that my job was on the rocks. In fact, those things could not have been further from my thoughts at that moment.

"Such a pretty girl," he growled, grinding his now-hard cock against me through our blue jeans.

I smiled.

"I've watched you at the shows, keeping everything moving ahead with your calm confidence. And perfect ass."

"Oh, god, you're embarrassing me."

"Really? Are you okay?" he asked.

I rolled my eyes and smiled. "I'm more than okay. In fact, I was thinking of getting a condom."

Cross's eyebrows snapped up. "Yeah? Well, I think that would be an excellent idea."

I wouldn't have minded jumping him right there on the sofa in my living room, but thought better of it. He stood to help me to my feet, and I led him by the hand to my bedroom. I fished around my jewelry box for a condom, which I tossed to him, and began to undress while he sat on the edge of my bed, watching my show.

First, I peeled off my jeans, having left my shoes behind in the living room. After I removed my long-sleeved T, I stood before him in my lacy bra and boy short panties.

"Turn around," he said in a whisper so quiet I almost didn't hear him.

I stared intently at him. "Yes, sir."

After I'd completed a full rotation, he nodded in approval. I wasn't sure where things were going, but I had a feeling I might like wherever we ended up.

"C'mere," he said, jerking his head toward the bed.

I approached him, slowly, giving him the chance to look me over. When I stood directly in front of him, he leaned back on his hands, and said, "Unzip me. Take out my cock."

Whoa. I got down on my knees because, god knew, I wasn't going to be steady on my feet with the hot need blasting through my veins. I reached for his belt and opened it, and with shaking fingers, fumbled with the button and fly of his jeans. When they were out of the way,

I gazed up at him. With a smile on his face, he nodded slightly.

I slowly pushed down the elastic waistband of his boxers and reached inside. I pulled out his enormous cock, wet at the tip from his precum.

And I felt my own panties getting wet.

I stroked him slowly, just with my fingertips, enjoying the velvety skin of his shaft.

"Do you want to suck me, Kealy?" he asked.

I nodded, unable to form words, so I tilted him toward me to run my tongue around his rim. He drew his breath sharply as his head lolled back.

Emboldened, I moved closer to the edge of the bed, between his legs, and lowered my mouth over him all the way to his balls until he bounced against the back of my throat. He groaned loudly.

"Fuck, baby, that feels good."

And I felt pretty damn good myself. In fact, I wasn't going to wait any longer. I let his cock bounce out of my mouth, and as I stood up, his head snapped forward to see why I'd stopped. When he figured it out, he smiled.

He stretched forward to lower my bra straps, then reached around for its hooks. His fingers dipped into the waistband of my panties, which he pushed to the floor where they puddled at my ankles. I was shaking with need for this man.

He sheathed himself with the condom, lowered his jeans and boxers below his ass, and held my hand as I climbed up to straddle him.

"Are you ready, darlin'?" he asked as he notched himself at my wet opening.

"I am, Cross. I want you to fuck me," I said as I lowered myself onto his length, trembling.

I barely felt the burn of being stretched wide enough to take him, and leaning forward, I kissed as we brought our hips together.

"You okay?" he whispered.

I pulled up to gaze directly at him.

"Yeah. It's so good, Cross."

With that, he held my hips in a vise-like grip and began pumping. I squeezed every inch of his cock as my pussy pulsed around him.

His aggression sparked my own orgasm, leaving me racked me with a powerful shuddering from head to toe. I grabbed his strong arms for purchase as he pounded his cock into me, lost in an uncompromising rut. His cock swelled one more time, and he groaned my name as he came hard, repeating it over and over again.

"Incredible," he murmured, his eyes still closed while he continued to shift inside me.

And it was incredible. Fucking incredible.

18

RAND

"I hate this goddamn makeup," I said.

"Yeah, but it makes you look so *pretty*," Shane said, smirking.

Marlon and Cross laughed.

"I'm serious. I don't know why we need to wear this shit. I look fine without it." I took another makeup remover pad and scrubbed until my face turned bright red.

It killed me, it really did, that they put this foundation crap on our faces to 'even out the skin tone' but gave us nothing to remove it with. So, I'd taken to carrying these makeup remover things they'd sold me at Sephora.

I'd gone in and totally pretended to be shopping for a girlfriend. I think they bought it, even when I asked for explicit instructions about how to use the things.

Whatever. I didn't give a damn whether they believed

me or not. But I sure didn't want to go to my night classes with makeup on, nor did I want any of my classmates to see that I carried makeup remover with me. I stuffed the package at the very bottom of my backpack under my textbooks. The only way they'd find it there was if I died and someone had to go through my stuff. And at that point, I guess I wouldn't really care.

"Dude, just go into the bathroom and wash your face with soap and water. That's what I do," said Cross.

But Cross was way more into the modeling thing than I was. He'd been at it since he was practically a kid, and nothing about it fazed him. I was just doing this shit to pay my way through school. Soon as I had my degree, it would be *adios* fashion world.

At least, that was the plan.

"I don't like the soap in the bathrooms here. It dries my skin," I said.

Marlon whooped with laughter.

Bastard.

"Rand, first you're bitching about wearing makeup, then you're saying the *soap dries your skin*. You need to man up, my friend," he said.

"Oh, fuck off, all of you." I was already in a shitty mood, having stayed up half the night studying for an exam I had in an hour.

"Chill, dude. You're gonna ace your exam," Marlon said.

I had to say, no one supported my education efforts more than Marlon, which was funny because he'd dropped out of school. But I supposed he'd go back some day when he was ready. At least, that's what he said.

"Okay, ladies," I said to the guys once we were back in our street clothes after another fashion show. "I'll see you later for beers. Wish me luck. And Shane, try showering this time before showing up."

"Just for that, Rand, I'm skipping my shower, and I'm gonna sit nice and close to you."

I laughed and headed out.

"MOM? THAT YOU?" I asked, fumbling with my cellphone earbuds.

"Oh, hi, Rand, honey. I was just looking to make sure your father was out back."

Now that I'd been away from the Bronx for a while, my mother's accent never failed to stun me when we hadn't spoken in a while.

"Mom, you don't have to hide from Dad that you talk to me, you know. It's not a crime," I said.

She lowered her voice, which pissed me the hell off. "Well, you know, I don't like upsetting your father."

"Oh, Mom." But what could I say? It was a conversation I'd had a hundred times before. The saying *hope never dies* carried a lot of truth.

"Hey, can you come down to the city and spend the day with me? I'd like to take you shopping and to lunch."

"Aren't you busy with your classes and your, um, work?"

"I am busy, but never too busy to spoil my favorite girl."

That got a giggle out of her, which was music to my ears. Shit, I'd do anything for my mom. She'd always believed in me and had run interference when things got rough with Dad.

Speaking of Dad…

"Is he there, Mom? Can you put him on the phone?"

"Oh, honey, you know how he is. And I think he might be busy out back…"

"Mom, please. Just tell him I'm on the phone."

She sighed. "All right. Hold on."

I heard her place the phone on the kitchen counter, the one I knew so well, I could picture every nick and scratch, and remember sitting on it when I was a kid getting my temperature taken. A door slammed in the background, which I knew was the one that led to the row house's back-yard. While waiting for my mother to return, I waved across the courtyard to a couple people from my history class. I could see from where I sat, the room was starting to fill up for the exam.

Funny how on exam day, the room was so much fuller than on a regular lecture day.

"Honey?" my mother asked.

"Yeah, Ma. Is he coming?" My chest was tight. Maybe I shouldn't have called right before an exam. It wouldn't do to go in distracted.

Another sigh. "Right now is not a good time, sweetie. He's trying to fix the fence we share with the Millers."

Eh. He was always busy with something. That was okay, though. I wasn't going to give up trying.

"I'm sorry, Rand. You know how your father is…" She trailed off.

"It's okay, Mom. Don't be sorry. But, I do expect you to find a day to spend with me. Will you think about it? I'd really like that."

"Yes, sweetie, I promise. I will. Seeing you would be good."

"Okay, Ma. I love you."

I heard a door slam in the background, and heavy footsteps in the kitchen.

"Bye now!" she said cheerfully.

As if she'd been chatting with one of her girlfriends.

A FEW HOURS, two cups of coffee, and a bag of peanuts later, I pulled open the door to the dingy bar we liked to call our home away from home. The guys had snagged our usual booth in the back, and there were already two sweaty pitchers of beer on the table.

"Dude. How was the exam?" Marlon asked, patting me on the back as I took a seat next to him.

All eyes were on me. "You know, I think I did pretty well. I'm really digging this early western civilization stuff. It's cool as shit. Now, I just have to write a paper."

"You're kicking ass, man," Cross said and raised his glass.

"Cheers to Rand." Everyone followed his toast.

"Thanks, guys. Now, what are you all smiling about?"

Cross set his beer down on the table, and leaned into the group.

"Rand, I was just telling Marlon and Shane. I am smitten by our lovely Kealy."

Did he really just say *our*?

"She's smart, ambitious, plucky, and of course, freaking gorgeous." He took a swig of his beer and wiping his mouth with the back of his hand, shook his head like he couldn't believe his luck.

Shane nodded. "I gotta agree with Cross here. I am smitten with the young lady, as well."

"Cool. I go out with her tomorrow night. Looking forward to it." And I was.

Marlon nodded, looking at the rings the beer had formed on the table. "I'll tell ya, Rand, she's something special. Pretty, intelligent…"

"Nice…" Shane added.

"I told her we wanted to help with her business," Cross said.

"Was she interested?" I asked.

He nodded. "Hell, yeah. But I think most of all, she was just really moved that we were interested in supporting her. I don't think she's had a lot of that in her life. You know, lucky breaks, that sort of thing. I told her, at the very least, we could all model for her."

"I'd give up my day rate for the lovely lady," Shane said.

Another round of *cheers to that* filled our table.

Actually, I think we'd all give up a lot more than that.

19

KEALY

I TOOK A DEEP BREATH AND STRETCHED UP TO MY FULL height.

"I know what you did," I said.

Muse looked at me like I'd just said the sky was falling in. "Excuse me?" He looked around, checking to see if anyone was listening.

I got it. He knew he had it coming and didn't want to be taken down in front of coworkers.

But humiliating him at work wasn't my style. I had a much better plan for getting even. All it entailed was a bit of patience, although that didn't mean I wasn't going to let him know I was on to him.

"You know what I'm talking about. And you won't get away with it."

He moved closer to me and gave me a look that made

my skin crawl. Had I really been best friends with this guy for two years?

How many signs had I stupidly missed?

"You know, Kealy—" he moved so close, I could smell the latte on his breath. "I always thought you were kind of, I don't know, naïve or something. Nothing personal, but if you want to make it in this business, you need to be a lot smarter about who you trust, and how you do your work."

"You are such a fucking asshole, Muse," I hissed.

But he just shrugged. "Maybe I am. But hey, who's Foster's pet right now, and who got the press coverage?"

I wasn't going to let that fucker taunt me. "You know what, Muse? You might have gotten those things but at what price? You're a thief and a liar? Are you proud of that? And don't think it won't catch up with you."

He rolled his eyes.

Could I be fired for smacking a co-worker? I decided I'd better not risk it.

"You see, you might think I'm naïve, but I've actually seen a lot. I know what happens to people like you. Scumbags like you. They get what they have coming to them. It might not be tomorrow, it might not be next week. But it will happen Muse, and when it does, I'll feel sorry for you. I'll just feel sorry for you."

For a moment, my words wiped the smug off his face, but it quickly returned. I wasn't surprised. He'd always been on the defensive side, able to justify what he wanted.

Obviously, a warning sign I'd missed.

"Until then, Muse, I'll bide my time as your meteoric

fall approaches. Because it will be here eventually. You can count on it."

I sauntered back to my desk, pleased at how I'd dressed him down without losing my shit.

It hadn't been easy.

RAND HAD INVITED me over to dinner that night, and I had to admit, I was more than excited to get to know the one guy in the group who I probably had the most in common with. I mean, we both came from difficult though not identical circumstances, and we'd each created a life for ourselves out of limited privilege. I gravitated toward people like that—there was a scrappiness to them I related to.

He buzzed me into his Upper West Side building just a few blocks off Central Park, and I wandered through a long hallway that smelled of his neighbors' dinners.

"Well, someone's come a long way from the Bronx," I said with a smile as he opened his door.

"Damn right. Now, get in here."

Taking my hand, he pulled me inside. The minute his door slammed, his arms were around my lower back and his mouth was on mine hard. Surprise gave way to an aching tingle between my legs that, if he didn't stop soon, would be desperate for relief. As if he could read my thoughts, he pulled back, his big earrings shaking, and ran his hands through my hair.

Shit.

"What can I get you to drink, beautiful?" he asked, leading me to the kitchen, where whatever he was cooking knocked me out with its delicious scent.

"This is gorgeous," I said, turning to take in the marble countertops, six-burner stove, and glass-fronted refrigerator. And because I could see right into the fridge, I spied some pink bubbles that I suspected he'd bought just for me.

"That looks good," I said, pointing.

"I thought you might like that," he said. "Myself, I'm enjoying a nice scotch. " He held up a rocks glass and shook it, rattling the ice cubes.

I settled onto one of the stools at the counter and watched him top off my champagne flute.

"So, how was the exam?" I asked.

He nodded thoughtfully and took a swig of his drink. "I think it went well. I'm loving the class. Western Civ," he said.

"Why don't you study history rather than business?"

He shook his head vehemently. "History will be a passion my whole life, no doubt. But growing up, I watched my dad struggle with his repair business. I want to know how to do things the right way."

I knew enough not to ask whether he and his dad would be going into business once Rand graduated. It was a pity his father couldn't be happy his son had taken a different path.

But kudos to Rand for bucking expectations. Letting

other people hold you back was the death knell to a good life.

"I admire how you've found your path and stuck to it," I said.

He walked around the counter to where I sat on a stool and positioned himself between my legs. "The same might be said of you, pretty girl."

A heat washed over my face. I'd always been prone to blushing, and the affliction got me at the worst times. Just when I was trying to be a cool girl...my face would knock me back down to size.

"Thank you," I said.

"Hey, I've seen what happens when you don't make a plan. All I have to do is look at my brothers."

"What happened to them?" I asked.

He leaned back against the marble on his elbows, and his strong pecs bulged against his plain white cotton button-up.

"Well, one is in prison. I can tell you that almost killed my mother. And the other is a deadbeat dad."

"And your father has a problem with what *you're* doing with your life? Oh, my god, he should build a pedestal and worship at your feet."

On one hand, people like Rand's dad infuriated me. But on the other, I supposed you just had to *walk on by*. Let their problems remain their problems...

I turned my head as Rand's front door opened. I almost fell off my stool.

Who should wander in...but Marlon. 'Course he looked

magnificent as ever with his shaved brown head and huge grin.

I looked between the two of them, and they just stared back at me in all their gorgeousness.

Damn them.

It didn't take long to figure out what was going on. And to be honest, I didn't mind at all.

"Yo, Mar, can I get you a scotch?" Rand asked as Marlon headed straight for me.

"Yes, *please*. Just what the doctor ordered. Although if I were a doctor, I might order this beautiful woman right here." He bent to kiss me so completely, I thought I might sway off my seat.

But when he stopped, I realized what I'd just done.

Kissed Marlon, in front of Rand. I wasn't sure how these guys worked, but that just seemed wrong to me.

"I'm sorry, Rand," I said, wiping my mouth as if that would undo it.

"Baby," Rand said, handing Marlon his drink, "it's perfectly okay that you kissed Marlon in front of me. It's not a problem. Is it, Mar?"

There wasn't even a hint of resentment on his face. I glanced over to Marlon, who just looked at me with his beatific smile.

Well.

I hopped off my seat and stretched my arms around Marlon's neck to continue our kiss. And wouldn't you know, it was hot as hell just *knowing* Rand was watching us.

And watching wasn't all he was doing. He walked up

behind me to smooth his hands over my blue jeans-covered ass. Through the denim, he grabbed fistfuls of my bum while his lips brushed the back of my neck. As he ran across my sensitive flesh, his hands found the front of my jeans and made quick work of my belt and fly. His fingers reached inside my lace panties and landed right on my swollen clit. My legs nearly gave out right then and there.

With the perfect amount of pressure, he circled my clit, sending lightening bolts of pleasure through every inch of my body. I held on to Marlon tighter, moaning into his mouth. He pulled back and looked at me.

"Mmmm. Baby's turned on, aren't you?" he teased.

I opened my eyes and gave him a sly smile. "A little. What about you?"

He answered by bringing my hand down to his rock-hard cock. I rubbed my palm against its length, and it was his turn to moan.

"Fuck, your hand feels good," he murmured.

"How you doing, baby?" Rand asked from behind me.

I leaned my head back so that it fell on his shoulder and twisted my neck to reach his lips.

"Yeah, look at our girl, Rand. She's hot for us both, isn't she?" Marlon growled.

I turned from Rand's mouth and nodded as I struggled for words. "Oh, yes. Both of you. Your hands...your lips..."

20

MARLON

DAMN IF OUR LITTLE KEALY WAS NOT ONE OF THE MOST smoking hot responsive women I'd ever had the pleasure of kissing. And if all went according to plan, there'd be a lot more kissing of her between Rand and me. We'd been friends a long time, the two of us, having met through the fashion show circuit. On more than one occasion, we found ourselves pursuing the same woman. Neither of us was the jealous type, though—so we'd decided to date the same girl, share her if you like, as long as she was open to it. And she often was.

I mean, what woman wouldn't want to have two men adore her? Or in the case of us guys, *four*?

And as Rand and I got to know Shane and Cross, they were intrigued by our unconventional arrangement when they learned of it. They joined us in dating the same women, at least until Cross had gotten married. We all made quite the team.

We shared. Just like a man-harem. The term made me laugh, it was so preposterous. But I had to admit, it came up, again and again.

And in all the 'arrangements' we guys had had over the years, I don't think any of us had been as smitten as we were by Kealy. By any measure, the woman was impressively beautiful and smart, but to see her in her element, practically running Forest's company—although god knew, she didn't get credit for it—made my dick hard every time I thought about it. And to be with her then, at Rand's, with her turned into putty in our hands, well, it didn't get much better than that.

Rand was still behind Kealy, working over her clit good. She was beginning to shudder, her eyes half-closed, and her orgasm was surely imminent as she held me with a death grip to remain upright.

I opened my own jeans so I could feel her on my cock, and when she wrapped her fingers around me, well shit, I almost blew my load right there.

But I didn't. I held it. I couldn't go before our girl. I wouldn't.

She ran her thumb over the head of my dick, by now trickling pre-cum. I went for her blouse buttons, and in moments, had pushed aside her lace bra to have my hands on her bare tits. When the air hit her lovely breasts, her nipples sprang hard and tight. I pulled on those pretty points until our girl moaned.

With Rand's hand working her pussy, she bucked her hips back into him, presumably to grind on his hard-on, and then moved them forward again to increase the pressure of his hand.

She moved her hand faster on my cock, her head hanging limp as her breath grew raspy.

"Oh…oh god…yeah…" she cried. "God yeah, fuck me Rand, I love your hand on my pussy, go baby, I'm coming now."

Her moans turned into screams, her head bucking so hard, her hair flew in every direction. She convulsed violently with orgasm, which threw me over my edge. My balls pulled in tight, and I tensed from head to toe. Roaring like I don't think I ever had, I spurted hot streams of semen into Kealy's hand.

She stroked me until I was dry, then put a finger in her mouth to taste me.

"Mmmm," she moaned, eyes still closed.

"You good, baby?" Rand asked quietly.

She attempted a weak nod as she turned and kissed him full on the mouth.

"Okay. Because now I'd like to fuck you," he said, running his tongue over her lips.

Her eyes were barely open, but she spoke clearly. "I want your cock. Get a condom."

Rand raised his hand, victorious. He was holding a Magnum that he'd fetched at some point, when I had no idea, because I'd been kind of busy, myself.

While Rand was getting ready, I helped Kealy out of the

rest of her clothes, lowering her jeans until she stepped out of them, and throwing her blouse and bra to the floor. All she was left wearing were her panties, which I pulled down to right below her pretty ass. I wanted to let Rand do the honors as he saw fit.

And Rand being who he was, always put a twist on his good times. Sometimes, I wondered if the guy ever fucked in the missionary position. The way *everyone else did it* was never the way Rand from the Bronx did anything.

He turned Kealy to face the marble counter and bent her forward until she was at a ninety-degree angle. He pulled her hands behind her back and held both wrists in one of his hands. With her panties just below her ass, she couldn't spread her legs. But that was okay, because with his free hand, Rand ran his cock between our girl's ass cheeks until he was good and wet from her juices. Like the hot little thing she was, she even raised her ass a bit to make herself available to him.

Christ, I thought I was going to blow another load. In fact, watching Kealy get worked over by Rand, I took my hand to my own cock, which was already rock-hard again.

He shifted his hips forward enough so I could tell he was starting to enter her. His grip on her wrists pretty much incapacitated her, leaving her with her head turned and cheek on the cold marble, ass waiving in the air.

Beautiful. Fucking beautiful. If I could, I would have taken a photo and used it to beat off every day for the rest of my life.

But I'd never take a picture of our girl. That is, unless she asked me to.

With a quick motion and a deafening groan, Rand buried himself in Kealy's pussy up to his balls. He held himself deep inside her, watching her face. Her breath came hard, and she mumbled nonsense.

Then, she exploded into another orgasm, as Rand just held his dick deeply inside her. While she was coming, he began to pump her pussy, quickly following her with his own explosion. As soon as he did, he released her arms and she clawed at the smooth marble for purchase. They convulsed together while I continued stroking myself. Fuck, that was hot.

First chance I got, I scooped her up and carried her to Rand's sofa. She burrowed her face in my shoulder as she came down from the good fucking we'd given her. I could have gone another round, but I didn't want to completely wear her out. In seconds she was snoring lightly in my arms. Not gross snoring, but cute girl snoring.

HOLDING Kealy while she snoozed was a sweet antidote to the earlier part of my day.

I'd called my dad. It hadn't gone well.

I don't know why I kept trying. He was pissed at me for not following in his footsteps. Nothing new about that. Insulted, I guessed, that I didn't want to be just like him. It wasn't enough. I wanted to be myself.

I guess that was why Rand and I were so close. We both had strained relationships with our dads.

"Marlon, good to hear from you, son." He was always cheerful at the beginning of the conversation, when he still had hope that his prodigal son was coming back to the flock.

"Dad, hi. How's Mom?"

"She's great. At the club right now, I think playing Bridge with the girls."

"So, Dad. I wanted to talk to you about a business venture." I wiped my sweaty palms on my jeans. Why did he have this effect on me? Shit, I was a grown man.

"Well, well! You know I love business ventures. I knew you had at least a bit of the family entrepreneur in you."

"Yeah, well, I hope so. Dad, through the business I'm in right now, I meet a lot of smart, ambitious, and talented people."

Dad guffawed loudly. Seemed he was relishing the new leaf he assumed I was turning over. "C'mon, son. Let me have it. You know a good businessman never beats around the bush."

God, he was a blow-hard asshole. Not to mention, completely lacking any ability for self-reflection. That's what happened when you went through life and no one ever called you out on your shit. It was like that when you had money. People suck up and after a while you began to 'believe your own press'.

"Yes Dad. You did always say that. Anyway, my friend

Kealy is starting her own men's wear collection, and I thought we might invest."

Silence.

"Dad? You there?"

"Marlon, did you say something about the apparel business?" he boomed.

Oh, Christ. "Yeah, I did. She's a very talented designer, and—"

"Okay, let me stop you right there. The Talbot family does not dabble in clothing, or anything else silly like that."

Unbelievable. And the smug jerk wondered why I ran away from him as fast as I freaking could.

"Well, Dad, I'm sorry to hear you feel that way, but I understand. Sorry to have bothered you—"

"Now, wait a minute, Marlon. You called to talk to me about investing in a fashion designer? I like that you're developing a head for business, son, but next time, please come to me with a real venture. One that is respectable and promises great profit margins."

And there we had it. *Respectable.* That was the word that was on the tip of his tongue our entire conversation, and which he was waiting, like a lion hunting his prey, to spring on me. As if he could kill me with it.

And in a way, I guess he did.

21

———

KEALY

Wait 'til I told Fantine.

Actually, I probably wouldn't tell her. She'd ask too many questions. And besides, this was all mine. At least for now.

Oh, to hell with that.

"Fantine," I whispered. I'd sneaked into Rand's bathroom with my cell phone. Someone had carried me to bed, and he and Marlon were now fast asleep. Guess I'd worn them out.

Yeah, right.

"Hey, Keal," she said in a sleepy voice.

I looked at the time on my phone. Oops. After midnight.

"Sorry, Fan, I just needed to talk to you for a sec."

Sheets rustled in the background, and I heard her propping herself up in bed.

"Keal, is everything okay?" she asked.

I pulled a towel around myself for warmth and sat on the edge of the bathtub. Rand's bathroom was about as fancy as one might expect, just like his kitchen. Too bad his parents wouldn't accept his financial help. Their lives would change, for sure.

"Everything's fine. Great, in fact. I'm staying over Rand's, if you haven't already figured it out."

"Oooh, my naughty little Kealy. Guess you did the nasty with your hot model, huh?" she teased.

"Actually…" I hesitated but then decided *what the fuck.* "I slept with him *and* Marlon."

She sucked in her breath so sharply, I thought she might choke.

"You did? You had a threesome? Well, you little ho. I love it. Can't say I've ever done that myself." She sounded a little wistful.

"I wouldn't worry, Fantine, you have your whole life ahead of you for threesomes and more."

"What do you mean *more?* Was anyone else there besides Marlon and Rand?"

"No. No, don't be ridiculous." Although, was she being ridiculous? Maybe that's what lay ahead for me.

She laughed. "I'm just pulling your leg. Sort of. So how was it? Everything you'd dreamed and more?"

"Shut up. Yes, it was awesome. I loved it. Super hot."

I heard footsteps in the hallway. "Fantine, I gotta go. Talk to you tomorrow," I whispered, swiping my phone closed.

I pulled the bathroom door open and walked *smack* into Marlon. But freaking naked.

"Hey, gorgeous. I thought I heard someone in there." He leaned against the doorjamb and smiled.

Damn him for being so good-looking.

"Oh yeah, just taking care of business," I said, smiling back. As exhausted as I was, I wouldn't have minded another round with him. Or Rand. Or both.

"Really? Taking care of business with your phone?" he asked.

Busted. "Oh I know. A terrible habit, isn't it? I take this thing with me everywhere I go."

Good save. *Right?*

"Okay, beautiful. Get back to bed. I'll join you there in a moment." He kissed my temple and closed the door behind himself.

I suddenly wasn't so tired any more.

"So...what do you think?" I asked, sitting back in my chair.

I looked around Marina's amazing house, the first one where I'd felt truly loved and truly at home. I'd come a long way from the few short years ago when I'd arrived there, eager to be a good nanny and make the Benson family happy. I never dreamed they'd give me so much more than I could ever repay them for."

Marina continued flipping through my sketchbook with all the care and respect she'd always shown my work and me. I was on the edge of my seat hoping she approved.

She nodded slowly and looked up at me.

Oh, god. She hated them.

"Kealy, these are amazing."

Shit. My eyes filled with tears, which I wiped away with my sleeve.

Marina laughed. "I've watched your work develop since you started fashion school. You just keep getting better and better."

There was no holding back. I gushed like a damn crybaby. "Th...thank you, Ma...marina..."

She patted my hand. "C'mon, now. You know you're good."

I blew my nose on the tissue she passed me and just nodded until the sobs stopped.

"Thanks, Marina," I said when my voice steadied.

"Let's go sit on the terrace," she said, letting me lead the way to a tiled patio with lounge chairs and a sprawling umbrella.

"When are the kids home?" I asked.

She glanced at her watch. "Soon. They had theater club after school."

She passed me a glass of lemonade. "What are you going to do with the designs?"

"Well, you know things have gone sort of sideways for me at work. I'm working on patterns, based on these sketches, and will start sewing samples at my kitchen table in the next few days."

"Oh, sweetie, that's so exciting."

I nodded, and the butterflies that had been making themselves at home in my stomach, returned. "Nerve-wracking, too."

"I bet. This is a big freaking deal. Going out there with your own collection. What will Forest say? And will you be able to pull it off?"

I grinned. "Good questions. It all remains to be seen. First, I believe Forest will be surprised but happy for me. Even thought he was bit a bit of an ass about the whole Muse fiasco, I know he supports people who leave the company to do their own thing. About pulling it off, well, yeah. There's that. I mean, it's one thing to create fifteen or twenty new designs and get them out there in front of people. But having the cash to produce the inventory to ship to the stores—that's another story."

And it really was. I'd heard the horror stories of up and coming designers, loved by the fashion press, who took orders from tons of stores, only to find they couldn't raise the couple hundred thousand dollars they needed to produce the garments they'd promised to ship. You didn't get a second chance when something like that happened. Too many burned bridges.

"Yeah, I'll be talking to some investors, for sure."

At least, that was the plan.

"Maybe I can help you, Kealy," Marina said.

The tears came rushing back. Dammit.

I shook my head violently. "No. I mean, no thank you, Marina. You've already done so much for me. I do know some people who might be able to help me with fashion shows and shoots, things like that."

"Of course, you do. You've been in the business now long enough to know all sorts of people."

I hesitated to tell her about the men. But not for long.

"I've met this group of guys. They're models and often work in Forest's shows and in his shoots. They want to help."

If she only knew…

"Well, there you go. And male models. Must be some nice eye candy."

What an understatement.

"You like any of them? Any romantic intrigue?" Marina had been gunning for me to get back into dating after the last asshole I'd been with.

"Um, yeah. I guess so."

"Yeah?" She leaned forward, excited out of her mind. "Which one? What does he look like?"

Shit. I just needed to spill it.

"Well, there's Shane, who is Irish with red hair and a crooked nose. Tall and thin. And then there is Cross, who has long blond hair he keeps in a man bun—"

"No, no, I mean, which guy is it who you like?" She was understandably confused.

"—and Rand has shoulder-length brown hair, earrings, and huge muscles. Last is Marlon. He is black, shaves his head, and dresses really preppy."

"Wow. What a collection. Which do you like?"

I took a deep breath. "All of them."

She threw her head back, laughing. "I bet you like them all. I like them too, from the way you described them."

"Marina, I really mean *all of them*," I said.

"Oh. Okay. Well, I guess, in time, you can narrow down your choice."

Time to be a bit more direct. "What I'm saying, Marina, is that I'm dating all of them. At least, at the moment."

Her eyes opened wide. "Well, you little vixen. You know, you're at the age when you should play the field. Good for you. How do you keep it secret from each of them?"

I sipped my lemonade. "I don't. They all know about each other. Sometimes I'm with more than one of them at a time, even."

She fell back in her chair. "No. Way."

I felt a blush moving its way over my face, which pissed me off. I didn't want to be embarrassed by my um…unconventional…arrangement.

"They share. They all date the same woman. They share her."

"No kidding. Wow. I've heard of threesomes, *ménage a trois*, but one woman *and four men*? Holy shit. How…does it work? It sounds kind of crazy."

"I'm not sure how it works. I'm just taking it day by day. I mean, I don't think it could be a long-term thing. I don't see how it would be possible. I want to end up with one, if one will have me. But it's early days, and I like them all. A lot. So we'll see what happens."

Yes. We would.

22

SHANE

THE ONLY WAY I COULD DESCRIBE HOW I FELT WHEN I SAW
Kealy across the bar was *soothed*. That's what it was. Seeing
her was *soothing*.

Christ, I was turning into a sap. But after the day I'd
had, I was desperate for her. I wanted to touch her, hear
her voice, smell the crook of her neck while running my
lips along her soft skin…

"Hey, baby," I said, sliding into a booth next to her at
our usual dive bar. She was a down to earth kind of girl, so
I had a feeling she would be fine with it. But I still had to
test her. It's what we guys did.

And so far, she'd passed every test with flying colors.

She planted her lips on mine, and there was an imme-
diate stirring in my pants. Her fingers ruffled through my
hair.

I liked that.

"Great place, Shane," she said, looking around. "I love a scruffy bar and a cheap beer. Look, we can carve our initials in the table."

She shot me a look. Was I being tested, now?

"We can do that. But what about the other guys? You know, Rand, Cross, and Marlon? Remember them?"

She blushed ever so briefly and shyly looked down at her beer. "I haven't forgotten them. How could I?"

She lifted her head to peer at me and perhaps make her point.

Which was good news. She was thinking of us all. Because we were all thinking of her.

"How was basketball tonight?" she asked.

It was an innocent question and sweet that she was asking after my day, but in spite of my best effort, my spine stiffened and my fingers tightened on my beer bottle. I started picking at the label with my other hand.

She seemed not to notice, and when the waitress lowered chicken tenders and fries before us, she eagerly dove in.

"God, I love fried food. I wish I didn't, but what's better than greasy saltiness? Mmmm," she murmured as she poured more salt on a piece of chicken and popped it into her pretty mouth.

"Fried food reminds me of Ireland." Funny how we Irish loved fried fish, and Americans loved fried chicken. They were both damn good, if you asked me.

"So…basketball…the community center? Remember?" She took a swig of her beer to wash down her fries.

God, I could fall for this woman.

"Yeah," I started, "it was a good practice. The kids worked really hard. Even made a couple of baskets." My gaze returned to my beer.

And she stopped chewing. "Are you okay?" she asked slowly.

I could see the concern on her face. To be honest, there was plenty to be concerned about. And it was high time I told her why.

"Did you notice that when you came down to visit me at the community center, I got us out of there in a hurry?" I asked.

She frowned. "Um, no. I didn't notice. Not at all. I thought it was just time to leave."

I nodded. "Yeah, it was time to leave. But there are good reasons. Once it starts getting dark in that neighborhood, I usually hightail it out of there. Actually, I always hightail it out of there once night falls."

"Oh. Well, I know it's not the best neighborhood, but I thought you felt comfortable there."

She was partially right. I *had* felt comfortable there. For a time.

"A few months back, I was heading out kind of late. I'd hung around with a couple other volunteers after our kids had left. On my way to the subway, I was jumped."

Kealy's eyes widened, and she sucked in her breath. "Oh, my god," she said softly.

I didn't want her feeling sorry for me. But she had to know about what had defined my nearly every waking hour since that dark night.

"They were kids. Well, not kids, but teenagers. I think it might have been a gang initiation type thing. There was a group of them. They took my wallet and then egged on a smaller guy."

"Egged him on to what?" she asked.

"Stab me. In the chest. They ran off, leaving me bleeding on the sidewalk. I am pretty sure they thought they'd killed me."

Kealy's voice caught, and her eyes got glossy.

Shit, the last thing I wanted to do was upset my girl, but she needed to know.

"Some passersby found me. Called the cops and got me to the hospital." I took her now-shaking hand and ran her fingers over the raised scar on my chest.

She smoothed her fingers over my shirt, and when she felt my scar, jerked her hand back, covering her mouth. Two heavy tears fell down her cheeks.

"God, I'm so sorry, Shane," she whispered. "And yet, you go back there. You're there all the time."

"I do. You're right. I didn't want to let them chase me away, and I didn't want to desert the kids. They already have enough challenges."

"So were they caught? Did the police find them?" she asked, dabbing her eyes with a napkin.

I looked across the bar, where I was always so at home. A shiver ran down my spine, anyway.

"Nope. But today, I saw them again."

"You *what?* You called the cops, right?"

"I didn't." Saying that out loud made me realize how crazy my choice to *not* call had been.

She looked at me like I was out of my mind.

I guess on some level, I probably was. "I didn't call," I continued, "because I want to take care of them myself."

Now, she'd really think I was out of my mind. Maybe I was.

She shook her head, "No, no, no. You can't do that. You have to call the police."

"I know you're probably right. But where I come from, you settle your own scores."

"Shane, you're not in a small town in Ireland now. You're in New York City. We have police and detectives to mete out justice. You should have called the cops. They could have arrested them."

"Yeah. I know. I just couldn't bring myself to do it. I was so angry they stole my health, my time, and my mental well-being. I was in bed for a month, first healing, and then having flashbacks, reliving it." My voice caught. Goddammit. But it felt so good to tell someone. And not just anyone. But my Kealy.

"You want to get out of here, sweetie?" she asked.

I looked down at her hand, which hadn't moved from mine in the time I'd been telling my story. "Yeah. Let's do it."

I threw some money on the table, and I waved at the bartender on our way out the door.

"I have to get up early, but I'd love it if you spent the night with me."

She hooked her arm through mine and stood on her toes to kiss me. Damn, I was captivated by this woman on a level that was all new to me. I wanted to get her home and fall asleep holding her, chasing away the unpleasantness of the day.

Of course, before we fell asleep, I might like to show her how much I liked her.

Our cab sped across town as we silently held hands. I was lost in thought, replaying the events of the day, and how when I saw my assailants, my heart pounded and it became hard to breathe.

God, I sounded like such a pussy. But shit, getting stabbed wasn't exactly fun.

My doorman buzzed us in, and as we walked through the lobby, it was clear Kealy was impressed. But she needn't be. I had nice digs because I made a good living. I was lucky. It was nothing more than that.

Our heels clicked on the tiled floor leading to my apartment, and we were silent until we were inside.

"Wow. This is amazing. And what a contrast to the bar where we just were."

I laughed. "You got me there. I like contrast in my life, I guess. Keeps my on my toes."

When I'd switched the deadbolt on my door, I turned to find Kealy just inches in front of me.

Perfect.

I took her hand and led her to my bedroom, where I

switched the lights on low and turned on Pandora. Then I turned to my girl.

But it seemed she wanted to take charge. No problem, there.

She pushed my leather jacket off my shoulders and lifted my T-shirt over my head. She paused long enough to kiss my scar. Then, with quick fingers, undid my belt and fly, my jeans falling to my ankles in a puddle. I kicked off my shoes to pull my legs out of my pants. My cock had sprung to attention in record time and was now tenting the front of my boxers.

Before she could go any further, I went after her top and pants. Damn if she didn't look amazing in a silky little thong and sheer bra. Good thing I hadn't known she had that get-up on under her clothes when we'd been out earlier. It would have been harder to concentrate than it already was.

She led me to my bed, where she pushed me down while removing my boxers. My cock bounced in the cool air, and then was engulfed by her hungry mouth. She went at me with such a vigor, I nearly blew my wad right then and there.

But I had self-control, if I had anything. I was going to lie back and enjoy watching my girl suck cock like there was no tomorrow.

Her lips bobbed around my swollen flesh and pistoned the length of my shaft 'til I was balls-deep in her mouth.

"Fuck…" I moaned.

Christ, she was amazing.

With her lips still around me, she looked at me in earnest. "Come in my mouth, baby. I want your cum."

Holy Christ, that did it for me. A rupture from the deepest recesses of my soul surfaced, as the most fucking amazing orgasm I think I ever had raced through me. I exploded in her mouth so fast and hard, she choked, and when she opened her mouth to breathe, my cum dribbled down her chin in the fucking hottest thing I'd ever seen.

But she wasn't done. She got back to sucking until she'd cleaned every drop of jizz off me. Then she crawled up next to me in bed and snuggled into my arms.

"Damn, baby. You just about killed me," I said.

She sighed beautifully.

If I wasn't so goddamn tired, I'd have another go.

"I'd never kill you," she murmured. "That would be stupid. How else would I get to do this again?

All right, then.

23

KEALY

"Coffee?"

I opened my eyes to a blinding sun. Well, I didn't really open them—I started to, and all I could do was blink furiously. I wasn't sure where I was, but I did know I was naked, my head pounding, and my mouth dry as hell.

Shielding my eyes from the torture burning into them, I looked around the strange room until my eyes focused.

A gorgeous man with red hair sat on the bed next to me. I looked up at Shane, wearing only blue striped pajama bottoms. And I saw his scar for the first time in broad daylight.

It was an angry red welt, not particularly large or scary to the eye, but it carried the weight of a life-changing experience. It had become part of who he was, and if he were to be in my life, it was to become part of who I was, too. I took a sip of the milky, sweet coffee he offered me and lightly ran my finger over the flaw in his otherwise perfect skin, more slowly and thoughtfully than I had the night before. I looked up at him.

"Yup. There she is. My beauty mark," he said with a laugh.

But I knew Shane was like me, and that in spite of our scars, whether inside or out, we were survivors. The years I'd spent bouncing around in foster care, being told kids like me never amounted to anything, left a scar just like his on my heart. I'd never forget it, but it wouldn't define me, either.

"I'm sorry you went through that," I said.

He nodded. "Thank you. I appreciate it."

I squeezed his hand and took another gulp of my coffee. "What time is it, anyway?" I asked, trying to remember where I'd left my bag, which would have my phone inside.

"Um. Looks like eight forty-five," he said, looking at the digital display on his stereo.

I leapt out of his bed. "Oh, shit. Oh, my god. Oh, shit. I'm going to be late for work." I began running around the room in a panic, collecting the clothes scattered all over the floor from our fun the night before.

"Slow down, cowgirl. Get yourself dressed, and I'll get you an Uber to work."

Fuck it. I'd have to wear the same clothes two days in a row, but I could probably change into something once I got to the office. There were all sorts of extra things just sitting around there, and Forest loved it when we wore his designs. I grabbed my things and raced into the bathroom.

"There's an extra toothbrush under the sink, darlin'," Shane called after me.

"Don't you have a shoot today?" I hollered.

"Yeah, but not 'til ten."

I rushed out of the bathroom. "Do I look okay?" I asked. "Presentable enough for work?"

He put his hand under my chin and turned my face as he lowered his lips to mine. His mouth felt like velvet, and my legs wobbled.

Shit. Did I really have to go to work?

Actually, yes, I did. It was a big day, and I had big plans.

Shane climbed in the Uber with me and dropped me in the garment district, where Forest's studio was. I watched the car pull away from the curb with him in it, on his way to making some photo look as perfect as he was.

OF COURSE, I ran smack into the boss the moment I arrived on our floor.

"Miss Rocher," Forest said with a smile and raised eyebrows, "we're starting in just a few minutes. See you in the conference room?"

"Be right there, Forest," I said, running to my desk to drop my things and grab my laptop.

We were meeting for our quarterly 'style out', where we

discussed the next season's concepts, and Forest provided direction.

Of course, Muse blathered on in the meeting, like he always did. It had never bothered me in the past, his desperate grab for attention—I'd thought it was an endearing little quirk. But now, it grated on my nerves to no end. So instead of listening, I thought about my guys and what might lie ahead.

They were all so great, with Rand working toward his degree, Marlon forging a path despite his father's resistance, Shane volunteering even after his horrible mugging, and Cross raising little Joey on his own. I was proud to call any of these guys my friend, and I was blown away by their interest in *me*.

Yeah, I'd come a long way from my yearly move from one foster family to another, lugging the few belongings I had from place to place in a dingy pillowcase.

"...and Kealy, I'd love to hear your thoughts," Forest said.

Shit. And don't you know, Muse sat there with a shitty smile on his face.

But I was prepared.

"I'm liking it, Forest. I think the military influence of this past season has worn itself out, and moving into something less trendy could be a really good move for us."

Forest nodded, considering what I'd just said. I stole a look at Muse, who was scowling. Not seconds before, he'd been pushing the military look. He'd probably never dreamed I'd contradict him.

But I'd never dreamed he'd fuck me over. So there was that.

And of course, none of them knew I had plans. Big plans.

I'd hummed my way through the rest of the day, on top of my game like I hadn't been in a while.

"Fantine," I said when she picked up on the first ring.

"Hey, stranger. Didn't see ya come home last night… again…" she taunted.

"You are right," I said, lowering my voice, "I did not make it home."

"And who were you with, this time?"

"Shane."

"And…?" she asked.

I thought back to his pain and thirst for vengeance. "He's awesome. Just amazing. And you should see his place—"

"Oh, my god. They're calling me. I gotta run."

"Okay, don't forget about tonight," I said.

But she was gone, off to another audition that would bring her one step closer to seeing her name in lights.

AFTER MY PRODUCTIVE DAY, I sneaked out of work early, feeling doubly guilty because I'd arrived late to begin with. But I had to get home for some fresh clothes and to put on a little makeup before meeting Fantine and her theater friends for dinner.

That was one of the things I loved best around New York. You could *never* run out of things to do.

I took the subway home, because that's how I rolled except for when I was terribly late and had to spring for an Uber or cab. I entered my apartment building and bounded up the stairs to the third floor, comforted by the familiar mustiness of the hallways and their tile worn bare from years of tenants coming and going.

When I put my key in the deadbolt, I realized it was open. Fantine must have come home, too, before the night's festivities.

"Fantine?" I hollered.

My heart made a thump so hard in my chest, it almost knocked me over. Our apartment was a mess, our belongings strewn all over the place. I looked toward the kitchen, and my biggest fear was realized.

My sewing machine was gone.

They say that when your home has been broken into, you're not supposed to enter, but instead, you should leave right away and call the police. I later wondered how many people followed those instructions, because all common sense left my little brain as I ran into the apartment to see if anyone was still there.

Thank god, no one was. Like I was going to take down a burglar? Right. But my fury at being invaded in such a way was so intense, I probably could have shredded someone with my bare hands.

At least, that's how I felt at the moment.

After a quick look around, and finding that the entire place had been pretty much ransacked, I wandered to the flimsy table where my machine had been.

Who steals a fucking sewing machine?

I grabbed my phone from my bag.

"Fantine?" I said in a shaky voice.

"Hey, you sound funny. What's up?"

"Fantine, someone broke into our apartment."

"*What?*" she said.

"You'd better come home."

"Oh, my god. I'll be there in fifteen."

I was close to a panic attack. It was bad enough someone had been in our place and made a mess of it. Honestly, we didn't have much worth stealing. Whoever went through the trouble to get in was probably pissed he or she'd bothered breaking into a place with no jewelry, money, or other valuables. But my sewing machine was everything to me, symbolizing when I really began to believe my life was permanently taking a turn for the better, and that I'd never go back to where I'd started.

Shit, my sketchpads.

The last time I'd been drawing was in bed. I raced into my bedroom and saw my latest notebook nearly all the way under my bed.

Whoever broke in had taken no interest in it, and instead, had just kicked it out of the way.

Thank god for little miracles.

That's when the tears started. What was it with life? Just

when you think you're getting ahead, there's always something out there to kick you right in the teeth and to remind
you that you weren't so special, after all.

24

CROSS

I swiped my phone open. "Hi Shane, what's up?"

"Hey Cross. I just wrapped up a shoot and found a text on my phone from Kealy."

"And how's the lovely Kealy today?" I asked.

"I'm afraid not so good. Looks like her apartment was robbed," Shane said.

"No shit. Christ." I'd been heading home but turned in the direction of Kealy's. "I'm going over there right now to make sure she's okay. I'll ask Joey's sitter to stay late.

"Sounds good, brother. I'll meet you there," Shane said.

Shit. As if she hadn't already been through enough.

She buzzed me in when I rang from the front stoop, and I took the stairs, two at a time. The door to her apartment was wide open and there were three police officers, walking around and taking notes, while Kealy and her roommate sat on the sofa with red eyes, holding hands.

What a shitty break. Even if they'd not lost anything valuable, the violation of having someone force their way into their home was enough to shake anyone to their core.

"Ladies, I just heard," I said, inching my way between the police officers and planting myself on the coffee table in front of the girls. I leaned to give Kealy a kiss on the lips and Fantine one on the cheek.

"My parents are coming to get me. They don't want me staying here any more." A sob caught in Fantine's throat. "Keal, you can come with me."

She shook her head violently. "I cannot move in with your parents." Her hand flew to her mouth as she realized she couldn't stay in her own home.

"Kealy, come stay with me. At least, for a few days while things get sorted out," I said.

Big tears rolled down her face, which she quickly wiped away. She wasn't the type to want pity, and the last thing I wanted was for her to feel patronized.

"Thank you. I may do that. Just for a few days."

We turned toward the door to see Shane rush in. He also planted a kiss on Kealy's lips and gave Fantine a big hug.

"Ladies, we've seen this sort of break-in before," a stout police officer said, interrupting our greetings.

"How'd it happen?" I asked.

He pointed toward a hole in the wall I hadn't noticed

when I'd walked in. It wasn't that large, but I could see straight out to the hallway.

"No way," I said.

"Yeah. When they can't get in through the door, if no one is at home in the building, they actually cut a hole in the wall to get in. You can't do that in the old lathe and plaster walls, but the ones that have been replaced with drywall, it's not too hard."

"No fucking shit," Shane said, examining the hole. "Who'd even think of such a thing?"

The cop shook his head sadly. "It happens. If there's a way to get in, thieves will find it. You ladies need to stay elsewhere while your landlord repairs the wall."

At that, Kealy's face crumpled. I knew she took pride in taking care of herself, and such a vulnerable position was torture for her.

The cops started to leave, and I turned to see another commotion at the door as a man and woman whom I guessed were Fantine's parents barreled in.

"Oh, baby, thank god nothing happened to you and Kealy," her mom said, wrapping her arms around her daughter.

After introductions, Fantine hustled to gather some belongings. Her mother turned to Kealy.

"You're coming with us," she said.

Kealy reached for her hand. "Thank you. I'm going to stay at Cross's for a bit, while the landlord makes repairs."

"Well, that's very nice of you, Cross," Fantine's dad said.

"Kealy, Fantine hadn't told us you had a new beau," her mom said, giving me the once-over.

Kealy looked between Shane and me and then back to Fantine's parents.

"Yes," she said, nodding. "I'm very lucky." She smiled at us both.

Confusion crossed Fantine's parents' faces. Her dad opened his mouth to say something but abruptly closed it when his wife bumped her knee against his. She smiled brightly. Hey, they were worldly New Yorkers. They'd probably seem arrangements much more unconventional than ours.

Although, it didn't get much more unconventional.

They said their goodbyes, and after several promises that Shane and I would look after Kealy until her apartment was habitable again, they left the three of us behind with the hole in the wall.

Shane reached for our girl's hand. "What did they take, darlin'? Anything important?"

Her voice wavered. "They got my sewing machine." She choked on a sob.

"Oh, baby, I'm sorry," he said, pulling her to him.

"I worked so hard to pay for that thing. I mean, I can always get another, but the good sewing machines are expensive. And just when I was about to get started on my samples." She looked down at her hands and shrugged. Discouraged, but not defeated.

Yep, that was my girl.

"All right," I said, ready for action. "Let's help you pack a few things, and we'll head over to my house. We'll figure out what to do about your sewing machine."

Kealy stood. "Okay. You know, my sketchbooks and fabric were not touched. So, in a way, the most important things I needed are okay."

"That's wonderful, love," Shane said. "Do you have some bags? We can gather all this and take it with us."

Kealy's eyes filled with tears again. "Thank you both. I can't tell you what this means to me."

I wanted to tell her I'd help her get another machine, but from what I knew, she'd chafe at any sympathy or charity. I'd help her all I could, of course, but knew to tread carefully. No one had seen what Kealy had, and no one really knew what could get in her way.

At least, not yet.

THE THREE OF us arrived at my place with duffel bags full of our girl's things. Shane had done his best to patch the hole in her wall, but until her landlord made a full repair, her apartment was open to pretty much whomever wanted in.

And while that was the case, Kealy certainly couldn't stay there.

"Is the boy still up?" Shane asked when we arrived at my place.

I turned to his nanny, who put a finger to her lips to quiet us, and shook her head *no*.

"Sounds like he's down for the count," I said. "But we can always check in on him." I gave the nanny cab fare and a hug goodnight. The woman was a godsend.

Kealy brightened up and said quietly, "Oh good, I want to see Joey. I want to see something innocent and beautiful." She followed me to his bedroom.

My heart swelled as we looked down at my little man. He was sprawled on his back like little ones often did, with his head turned to the side. This showed off his profile of a tiny pug nose, double chin, and lips that fluttered with every exhale. Perfection.

When I watched him, I exploded with love. I mean, it broke my heart knowing he wouldn't grow up experiencing his mother's love. And even though he'd eventually ask questions about her dying, I was prepared to be the parent he needed and deserved. I pushed my sad feelings for him aside and thought how lucky we both were that Kealy had stumbled into our lives.

My only hope was that she stuck around, for not only me and Joey, but all the guys.

"Look at him!" Kealy exclaimed, gazing down at Joey. "Such a perfect thing to look at after today's fiasco. Makes me remember there are good and beautiful things in the world."

Yeah, I was also thinking of things good and beautiful. The Kealy kind of good and beautiful.

I turned to her. I'd been waiting all freaking evening. Shane stood just behind her in Joey's dim bedroom.

"C'mon, baby. Let's keep Joey asleep so we can have some adult fun."

She gave me the sexiest freaking smile and took my hand.

Hell, yeah.

She turned to Shane and took his hand, too. We both followed her out of Joey's room, back to my living room.

"Sit down," she said, gesturing at the sofa.

We weren't fools. We followed her instructions.

"I want to thank you two for all your help this evening. It's been hard, and will continue to be for a while, but you're making it more than bearable. In fact, I've nearly forgotten about my losses. Now that I'm out of that apartment with the hole in the wall, I'm not sure I really lost anything. Well, not anything of value, anyway."

"I love it, baby. You are fucking tough," Shane said, his Irish accent making him sound extra badass.

Personally, I couldn't be with someone who wasn't resilient, just like Shane couldn't. Life threw shit your way no matter who you were, and there were two kinds of people. Those who got up again and those who didn't.

And I knew which club we all belonged to.

25

KEALY

WHAT A NIGHT. OH, THE CONTRASTS. FIRST, BEING devastated that someone invaded my home.

And then, spending time with Shane and Cross. Well, shit, if that didn't remind me what was valuable in life, I didn't know what would. I loved those guys.

Oof. Did I just say *love*?

Ohmygod. I was falling. And hard.

And there they sat, right in front of me. Two of the most freaking gorgeous and amazing men I'd ever known. On a sofa. Just before me. They were mine, all mine.

At least, for a little while. And I was going to enjoy every second.

"Well, guys," I said, swaying a bit with my hands on my hips. "I'm trying to think of what I might do to show you my appreciation for your support tonight. I mean, if you hadn't come by and swept me off to this awesome place to stay, I would have had to go home with Fantine."

They both laughed. I was glad I could be funny after everything that happened.

I walked up to my guys, sitting next to each other on the sofa and put a hand on the side of each of their faces. Where to start? Shit.

But I needn't worry about that. They both stood and in a moment, I was sandwiched between the two.

Hands reached to pull my top over my head, and another pair lifted my skirt. They inched me toward the sofa, where I was directed to get up on my knees. I reached for the sofa back to steady myself as my lacy boyshorts were first pulled to my knees and then down over my feet. Hands —I wasn't sure whose—smoothed over my ass, cupping squeezing, and pulling my sensitive flesh until I instinctively arched my back to open myself and give them more.

"Fuck, yeah," Cross growled. "Look at our baby."

"Beautiful. Just beautiful," Shane murmured.

Someone's fingers traveled down my pussy until they parted my lips, drawing moisture from my clit to ass and back. I was so exposed, the way I was offering myself to both guys, but I felt safe and adored.

Shane, I think it was, positioned himself next to me, with one foot up on the sofa, and one remaining on the living room floor. I turned my head toward the sound of his zipper opening, and his rigid cock presented itself, right next to me. I turned toward him, and he held it and directed it gently between my lips. I clamped down on his swollen head, savoring the early taste of his cum, hoping he'd give me more later.

Cross, still positioned behind me, must have knelt because I felt his hot breath between my legs. Two fingers opened my lips, and his wicked tongue crammed itself into my core, leaving me shrieking as best I could with a mouthful of Shane's cock.

Hadn't I just been with two guys? Yup, I had, and now I was back for more. And god, I loved it. And all I could think of was how much I wanted more, like some sort of addict.

Shane continued to push into my mouth, so I focused on relaxing my jaw to take as much of him as possible. Cross lowered his tongue to zero in on my heavy clit. When he did, in spite of the trembling legs I was kneeling on, I pushed back into his face, not caring that I was also shoving my ass right into him. All I could think about was relief, and one of the best ways to get that was to have him suck my clit, and suck it hard.

While I hungrily devoured Shane, I arched into Cross to intensify the sensation of him eating me. Fuck, I wanted more, and I wanted it harder and faster. Didn't he know that?

Turned out he did, because while he sucked my poor clit, he drew my slickness up to my asshole and began to press against my opening there. I'd not been invaded in that way, and never thought I would be, but with both of these amazing men at my feet, well, I didn't care what the hell they did to me. It was all good. In so many ways.

After pressing on my asshole with his thumb, Cross entered me a scant inch. The sensation nearly drove me wild, and when he pushed further inside me, I realized I was desperate for him to fuck me. It had been a crazy night, and I just wanted to forget. I needed to forget. And he knew what that was like.

As did Shane.

I let the cock fall out of my mouth. "Do you have a condom?" I muttered, not entirely sure anyone would hear me, but hoping someone did.

"Go get a condom, man," Shane said as he lowered his mouth to mine.

His tongue pushed between my lips just as his dick had done a moment before. But this tasted completely differ-ent, kind of minty instead of salty, and oh so intoxicating. His lips massaged mine, his tongue tickling me until I was moaning with the pleasure of his attention.

I'd almost forgotten about Cross until I heard him sheathing himself. He ran his cock up and down my slit, getting himself nice and wet. His thumb returned to my ass, and for a moment, I was afraid he was going to take me there.

I'd never done anal. I wasn't sure I wanted to. But his thumb felt so fucking good.

But it turned out anal would have to wait for another day, because the engorged head of his cock notched itself at my pussy opening while his thumbs pulled open my swollen lips.

"Are you ready for me, baby?" he snarled.

I couldn't speak. So I nodded.

Cross entered me with a slow but steady pressure, filling me beyond capacity and then some. I tried to shrink away due to the initial sensation of discomfort, but he had a hold on my hips, and there was no moving at all. In about thirty seconds, I realized I didn't want to.

I pushed back against the length of his cock 'til he was balls-deep. Something began to roar through me, like an approaching train. Shane's cock was back in my mouth, and my hand flew to work my clit. My eyes must have fallen closed because all I knew was sensation streaming from my core to my extremities. I shook from head to toe, and when I started to come, I was one violent convulsing ball, begging for more. A groan erupted from behind me as Cross blew his load, quickly followed by Shane, who emptied his seed down my throat. I swallowed all I could, a little dribbling onto my lips.

I was ready to collapse on the sofa when strong hands lifted my shaking body and guided me to a bed. They tucked me under a fluffy down comforter and kissed my forehead. Someone crawled in behind me and spooned my limp form. Whoever was in front of me pushed my hair out of my face and reached for my hands.

Just a few hours earlier, I was bemoaning my ill fortune. And now, I was thrilled about my riches.

I HAD no idea how much time had passed, but something startled me awake at a time I couldn't determine. It was still dark outside, and I didn't want to wake my guys, so I didn't move. But I did feel them on either side of me, their soft breathing bringing a peaceful rhythm to the dark and settling my heart into a soft and steady beat.

Okay. There was no denying it. I was smitten, plain and simple. Done. It was all over. I couldn't deny it.

Cross, Shane, Marlon, and Rand. My guys. I had to choose, I knew that. But until I absolutely had to, I'd enjoy every second with them.

I knew you didn't get this kind of luck more than once in your life. And I wasn't letting it go any time soon.

26

RAND

I found out about Kealy's break-in from Cross the next day at a shoot for Ralph Lauren. As usual, it was hot as hell under the lights, which was melting the makeup I already hated so much. They had to keep stopping to mop me up.

"Dude, how is it you always sweat so much?" Cross whispered. There was a female model between the two of us, but she didn't speak English.

"I know, right? Sometimes I wonder how I even keep getting these jobs."

The makeup guy slathered another layer of powder on my face. If the shoot didn't end soon, the stuff would start to landslide off my face in chunks.

Just then, the stylist brought over a nice, heavy winter

jacket for me to wear on top of my already too-hot Fall ensemble.

Were they out of their fucking minds?

But I just nodded and shrugged the jacket on. It'd be over soon, and I'd walk out of there with a fat paycheck.

I just had to keep reminding myself of that.

Plus, my mind was full of thoughts of our girl. I couldn't wait to reach out to her and hear her voice. I know she was okay because my buds had stepped up to the plate and taken care of her, but I had to hear it with my own ears.

Christ, I was turning into a pussy.

Another wardrobe change had me in a tux with the same non-English speaking woman as before, who was wearing a silk gown cut to her navel. She was stunning, no doubt, but like all female models, far too thin for my tastes. I wouldn't have minded seeing that dress on the beautiful Kealy.

In fact, maybe I could get it for her.

The moment the shoot was over, I was in the makeshift dressing room for the male models and called her.

"Sweetie. Holy shit, Cross told me what happened," I said.

"Can you believe it? I can't even stay in my place until the landlord repairs the wall. And Fantine's parents want her to move home."

"I heard they got your sewing machine."

"Yeah," she said in a shaking voice. "I'm trying not to think about it."

God, it sucked to hear her unhappy. I wished it had been me who'd been robbed.

"Hey," I said, looking at my watch. "I just finished my morning shoot. How 'bout I come by the office and take you to lunch?"

"Oh, that sounds great," she said, perking up a bit.

Not twenty minutes later, I was in the lobby of Kealy's building, cooling my heels and watching the lunch crowed stream out.

"Rand!"

I looked up to see none other than Muse, the bowtied dickhead who screwed over Kealy, grinning in my face like we were buds. For a moment, I thought of decking him, the way we'd handle things back in my Bronx days, but time and maturity had taught me there were much better ways of getting even with the fuckers of the world.

So, I stuck out my hand.

"Oh, hey. How're you doing?" I asked.

"Heading out for lunch. It's that time of day, you know!" he said cheerily. "Speaking of which, what are *you* doing here? We're not having fittings this week, are we?"

I shook my head. "Nope, no we're not."

I debated telling him I was there for Kealy, but thought better of it.

"Well, it was good seeing you, Muse," I said, looking past him to let him know he'd been dismissed.

He stood before me smiling for a moment until it sank in that our conversation was over.

"Well. Okay. I'll see you around."

He disappeared out the door and onto the crowded Manhattan sidewalk.

I watched dozens more fashion-types walk by since I was in a building full of designers and their teams, nodding to the folks who looked familiar from the show circuit. But when a warm hand landed on my arm, it was like no one else was around.

Kealy popped up on her toes to lay a hungry kiss on my lips.

I knew how she felt. When things got rough, it was normal to crave physical closeness. 'Course I hoped she'd crave physical closeness with me, regardless of whether or not her apartment had just been broken into…

"Just saw your buddy, Muse," I told her while I wrapped my arms around her and buried my nose in her delicious hair.

"Ugh, that creep," she said as we unwound ourselves from each other.

Damn if she wasn't adorable in some wide-legged pants with a small bib on the front. Reminded me of a sailor or something like that.

"What sounds good for lunch?" I asked.

She looked around and then up at the day's beautifully clear sky.

"You know what I would just love? A hot dog from my favorite corner vendor, and then to sit in Bryant Park.

I knew I loved this girl.

Oh, shit. Did I say love?

Settled onto a shady park bench only a few minutes

later, we were armed with two dogs each, both loaded with the works—ketchup, mustard, sauerkraut, and grilled onions. Kealy the badass had even opted for hot peppers. I was impressed my girl could down two of New York's favorite vendor treats, and eat them as spicy as they came, at that.

"Oh, my god, this is so good. Just what I needed," she moaned as she balanced her food on the napkins barely covering her lap.

"So what are you going to do about your apartment?" I asked.

Something dark passed over her face, and I regretted bringing it up.

But hey, I wanted to offer my support, not pretend like it never happened.

"Are you gonna stay at Cross's for awhile?"

"He invited me. But I don't want to impose. I mean, he has Joey and all...it could get crowded."

I raised my eyebrows. "Are you serious? I've seen his place. It's freaking huge."

"I know, I know," she said, nodding. "I guess what I mean is that I don't want him to *feel* crowded, in spite of the extra space he has."

"Darlin', he wouldn't invite you if he didn't want you. But if you're not down with staying at his place, you could always stay at mine." I didn't mean to cock block my buddy, especially since we were into sharing, but wasn't it just common courtesy to offer our girl options?

Eh. I was an asshole.

"Look, Kealy. We want to help you in any way we can. Your happiness is ours."

She looked a little flustered at the word *ours*. It was cool, though. To be expected, and all that.

I continued before she could protest. "The guys and I have been talking."

She frowned. "Huh? What about? Why?"

I reached for her soft cheek and smoothed my hand over it. "We want you to know you don't need to go back to that apartment, ever, if you don't want to. Stay with us. Any of us."

She sat back hard on the park bench, biting her lower lip. "I can't do that. I mean, thank you, Rand. I'm very grateful. To all of you. But I have to make it on my own. And…"

Why did she trail off?

"Yes? What's on your mind, baby?"

"I can't date multiple men. I want to be with one person. One person who wants to be with me."

My heart fell for a second, but it was all good. Most people wanted to be with one other, and her preference would come as no surprise to any of us.

"I respect that. We all do. And we'll support any decision you make." It kind of killed me to say that, but supporting her, however much disappointment might come along with it, was the right thing to do.

"I appreciate that. It's hard. I mean, well…I've become attached to all of you. You're so different from each other but also so amazing. And the fact that you're friends…"

"I guess that makes it harder, and easier, all at the same time," I said.

She looked at me, and damn if she didn't have tears in her eyes. It kind of broke my heart. She asked for so little and deserved so much. And we guys wanted to give her all we could. Make up for her shitty past.

I turned to face her straight on. "Why don't we all get together tonight? All five of us? Well, Cross might need to bring Joey, but he doesn't eat much."

That got a chuckle out of her.

"We could do that," she said slowly. "Yeah, that might be a good idea. I'd love to cook for you all. But I guess I can't do that now with my busted up apartment."

I wondered for a moment if I could talk her out of going back to her office and into coming home with me to spend the afternoon in my bed.

But there would be time for that sort of thing later. At least, I hoped so.

27

KEALY

"I heard about the break-in."

I looked up from my computer to see Forest pulling up a chair to sit beside me.

I sighed deeply, for about the tenth time that day. "Yeah. It's a drag. I mean, they cut a hole in my wall. Can you believe that?"

He shook his head. "I'd heard of that before, thieves cutting their way into someone's apartment. But I'd never known anyone it happened to."

"Well, let me be your first," I said with a small laugh.

He shook his head. "I'm so sorry."

I'd been on the verge of tears since lunch, when Rand told me that he and the guys wanted to do whatever they could to help me. I hadn't had many people like that in my life. But I guess you don't need many. A few is all it takes.

And now, Forest's compassion was moving me to tears, literally. "Thank you, Forest," I said, sniffling and quickly wiping my eyes.

"I heard about your sewing machine and wanted to offer you the extra one we have in storage. It's barely been used and is yours whenever you want it," he said.

Well, that was all it took. My chin quivered as hot tears ran down my face. I covered my mouth with my hand to stop any noises that might escape—it was one thing to cry in front of Forest, but I didn't need to entertain the rest of the office.

"Y…you don't have to d…do that, Forest," I said, trying to get my emotions back under control. In spite of my recent disappointment in him, he really was a good guy.

"I know I don't have to. I want to," he said. "You work your ass off for me, Kealy. Don't think I don't notice. This is one small thing I can do for you, and I'm happy to."

"Th…thank you, Forest." I blew my nose and dabbed my eyes. I was back.

And a freaking *new* commercial sewing machine?

He patted my shoulder. "You're welcome, kiddo. And thank *you*."

Wow. Sometimes life crapped on you, but sometimes, you came out cleaner than before.

THE DAY FLEW by as I got the bits and pieces of my life that had been thrown off track by my burglary back in order.

Marina had agreed to let me set up her guest room as a sample-making studio until I was settled either back into my old apartment or found a new one. I'd head over there the following weekend with my new machine courtesy of Forest, my pattern-making supplies, and the piles of fabric that the robbers had thankfully either not noticed or not been interested in.

Even my landlord was coming through for me. He'd boarded up the hole in the wall so no one could get in and promised to have it permanently fixed in the next couple days. He was giving us one month free rent.

Everything was falling into place. Well, almost everything.

The *guys*. All four of them. What the fuck was I going to do about them?

If I were honest with myself, I was into them all.

Maybe I was even falling for them a little.

Okay, maybe even a lot.

Shit.

Marlon was so goddamn hot with his shaved head, long curly eyelashes, and glossy brown skin. He was finding his own path, which I had so much respect for.

Rand, with his messy, Nirvana-type hair, tattoos, and earrings was my Bronx bad boy. Except there wasn't a single thing bad about him. The way he looked after his mom and tried to have a relationship with his father made my heart swell.

Shane, my Irish red head with his crooked nose and sky-high height. The scar on his chest reminded him every day that someone had gotten the better of him, but only for a moment in time. I knew he'd eventually put those demons to sleep.

And then, Cross, my blond man-bun wearing honey. Losing his wife like he did might have done in another man. But he had to step up to the plate for his little guy, and he did it with a dedication that brought tears to my eyes.

How in the hell would I ever choose one? How would anyone choose one?

Why couldn't just one of them have liked me?

Oh, right. That wasn't how they rolled.

But surely, they'd let me be happy with just one of them. I thought back to Marina's confusion when I'd tried to explain the whole concept to her. No, I couldn't be with four guys. That was just too weird.

So, after work, I headed over Rand's for dinner with a bottle of wine in my hand. I wasn't sure how the evening would go, but it didn't really matter since I'd made plans to stay at Marina's.

The big sis I never had, that's who Marina was to me.

I crossed Rand's magnificent lobby, my heart pounding. When I exited the elevator, Marlon was standing in the doorway, waiting for me. It was all I could do not to run to him.

Oh, fuck it. I ran to him anyway, jumping in his arms. He twirled me around in Rand's foyer, where Shane found us in a lush kiss.

"Mmmm-mmm. That looks mighty hot," he said in a low voice.

I jumped back from Marlon, with the kind of heat washing over my face that I knew meant I was blushing like an idiot.

"Darling," Shane said, "you do *not* have to be embarrassed."

He hooked a finger under my chin and raised my mouth to his, laying an equally hot kiss on me.

Well, then.

Focusing on dinner was not going to be easy.

I poked my head into the kitchen and found Rand and Cross deep in conversation about New York sports teams and their coaches. But as soon as they saw me, they went silent. Their gazes running over me turned my legs to jelly, forcing me to steady myself with a hand on the countertop.

"Hey," I said, trying to act cool and collected, but knowing I was probably bombing, miserably.

"Hey?" Cross said. "Is that all I get?" A giant smile spread across his face.

I ran to throw my arms around him. How could I not? I loved this man.

I loved them all, actually.

Shit. What a mess.

I turned to Rand and greeted him with the same enthusiasm.

"Bubbly?" he said, handing me a flute.

I pulled up a barstool next to Cross and was flanked by the other two guys.

"You know me so well," I said after a sip of heavenly champagne.

"Yeah, I guess I do," Rand said with a wink. "I guess we all do, on different levels."

"What'd you make us for dinner, man?" Marlon asked.

"You'll see. In fact, head on over to the table, and I'll bring out the grub," Rand said.

But it was hardly grub. Christ, a gorgeous man who could *also* cook? This was dangerous.

He appeared with a large ceramic dish and served us what was probably the most incredible lasagna I'd ever had. The noodles melted in my mouth, and his homemade tomato sauce was better than anything I'd had in any Italian restaurant in New York—and that was saying a lot in a place with an Italian joint on just about every corner.

The dining room was silent for several minutes as the guys devoured their meals. I couldn't blame them—I wasn't speaking, either, that's how good it was.

So I jumped at the opportunity to speak to all of them at once.

"Guys," I said, taking a deep breath. "I want to say something to all of you. I pushed my chair back and stood for emphasis. It must have worked because everyone put his fork down and gave me his full attention.

"Thank you for being so awesome about supporting my dreams to be a designer on my own, and especially for helping me through the break-in of my apartment. You've all been so generous and kind."

I looked down at my champagne for a moment.

"Really, I'm not sure I deserve all this."

"Kealy—" Marlon started.

"Wait, wait, Marlon. I have to finish, first."

He nodded and sat back in his chair.

Fuck, just say it.

"I don't think I can be shared by the four of you. I just don't think it would work for me. So, if it's okay with you, I'd like to choose one of you. I'm not sure how I'll do that, but I care about you all, and I hope at least one of you feels the same way towards me."

"Kealy," Rand said, "you don't have to do this—"

"But I do, Rand."

They looked around the table at each other, and in spite of my just having finished dinner, the pit in my stomach grew.

I was going to be responsible for hurting some, or maybe even all, of these men.

28

MARLON

All right. Kealy was tripping on the sharing thing. It was to be expected.

It wasn't easy to be unconventional. I knew that first-hand. Coming from a family like mine and not following everyone else's footsteps into the world of movers and shakers, floored my parents. My dad would judge me for the rest of my life.

Which just goes to show, you can't live for someone else. Kealy had to do what was right for her. Whichever way she went, we'd support her. Of course, I knew what I hoped she'd do.

But it was her choice.

"I'm sorry," she said, plopping back down at the dining table where the rest of us had put down our forks—something we never did when we'd been served Rand's lasagna.

"Don't look so sad, baby," I said. "I brought you some good news tonight."

As all eyes spun in my direction, I caught a spark of hope in Kealy's beautiful green eyes. I had to love that about someone who, in the face of hard times, kept looking for the silver lining.

I hoped I could get her the silver lining she deserved.

"I can fund your start-up," I said simply.

Her mouth opened slowly, then closed just as slowly.

Rand whistled softly. Wasn't sure what that meant. But, honestly, I was focused on my girl.

Our girl.

She shook her head quickly, throwing her blonde hair all over her face. "No. No, I can't accept something like that."

I said nothing, giving her time to run through all the possibilities. She'd clearly leapt at turning down my offer, a knee-jerk reaction I'd half-expected. She was proud. She wouldn't want charity.

But this wasn't charity. It was a business proposition, and from what I knew of her work, and the fashion industry, it was a *smart* business proposition.

She picked up her fork and took a mouthful of lasagna.

She was a stubborn one, apparently.

"Kealy, don't you want to hear about what Marlon has in mind?" Cross asked. I eyed him across the table with the slightest nod of thanks.

I needed my brothers' support to convince our girl to accept help.

She didn't look up from her plate. "It's…um…weird. I couldn't do that. I don't even know what's going to happen among all of us. How could I let you get involved with the collection I want to create?"

And when she finally did look at me, I saw torment on her beautiful face. That about killed me. But I stayed silent. I was nothing if not patient.

"Love, if I could speak for Marlon, I think he's trying to say he believes in you," Shane said.

"Just tell me you'll think about it," I said. It was a lot to take in. I knew that.

A small smile grew on Kealy's face. "Thank you, Marlon. You're so incredible." She looked around the table. "You all are, really. So amazing."

"We think the same of you, doll," I said.

"On that note," Rand said, rising from the table, "let's retire to the living room for some after dinner drinks."

Rand's place had killer views of Upper Manhattan, all the way to Harlem and beyond. We grabbed seats where we could enjoy the city so far below us, while he poured us guys some scotch. Kealy surprised me by taking one, too.

"I'm going for the hard stuff, guys," she said, raising her glass in toast.

Got to love a woman who drinks scotch.

Rand went over to his stereo, where he turned Pandora to the Buddha Bar station. Sexy world music filled the room. Kealy's shoulders relaxed as the tension she'd been carrying withered. Christ, she might be able walk away, but

I was getting to where I didn't think I could breathe without her.

Cross had taken the sofa seat next to Kealy and brought her hand to his lips. He brushed them over her soft skin, and she dropped her head back, letting her eyes flutter closed.

Fuck, it drove me crazy to see her getting turned on. I shifted in my seat to take some of the pressure off my growing cock. Shane saw me doing it and stifled a laugh.

Fucker. If he wasn't hard yet, he would be soon.

"How you feelin', baby?" Cross asked, taking Kealy's drink from her and setting it on the coffee table.

She looked up. "Awesome, really. It feels to good to be here with you guys." She looked at us all, one by one.

"Yeah? How would you feel about standing up for us and taking off some of your clothes? Not all of them. Just some." He'd always been an instigator. Loved that about him.

She shrugged shyly, but the smile on her face screamed she was game.

"Well, I don't know about that, Cross. I mean, would you respect me in the morning?"

Christ, her mood had improved.

Cross threw his head back and laughed. He then reached for our girl and pulled her to him. Their lips crashed together with a fury that about killed me.

I crossed the room in double time, took the other side of the sofa from Cross, and turned Kealy to kiss me.

Cross's face broke into a huge smile when she began to work the buttons on her blouse.

"Stand up, baby," Shane said, gently pulling her from me to get her standing. I remained in front of her and returned to our kiss, as he opened her jeans. Together, he and Cross shimmied them down her hips. Her shirt fell to the floor at the same time, leaving her wearing nothing but black lace panties that rose over her ass cheeks just enough to expose her beautiful little globes of flesh.

I was an ass man; I had to admit it.

I immediately knelt behind her, covering her bum with little kisses and bites. Every time I put my teeth to her, she tensed a bit and then relaxed, leaving her cheeks dancing with little wobbles.

It was more than I could take.

I pushed the black lace of her panties deep into the crack of her ass and opened her cheeks, pushing my face as deeply between them as I could. I took a deep inhale of her musky scent and nearly exploded in my jeans when she pushed back into me.

Shane had moved in to kiss our girl, his hands cupping her lovely face. With her blouse out of the way, Shane helped himself to her gorgeous tits. Her nipples were by now bright pink from his attentions, and not to mention, very prominent.

Rand, who I could see from my perch between Kealy's lovely ass cheeks, had been watching us all from across the room. Wearing a contented smile, he had one leg crossed over the other, his arms resting on the easy chair as he jangled the ice cubes in his scotch glass. He looked just like an ad I'd seen earlier in the day for an expensive brand of liquor. Actually, it *had* been him, when I thought about it. Modeling was funny that way. You'd be surfing the internet and come across an ad picturing someone you'd just worked with the week before.

Or someone you shared a beautiful woman with.

He took one more swig of his drink, set it down, and crossed the room to the sofa, where he took a seat and ran his hands up and down his thighs.

"C'mere, pretty," he said, crooking a finger at Kealy.

The three of us currently working her over—Cross, Shane, and myself—released her and watched her go to Rand.

As she positioned herself right before him, he hooked his hands in the waist of her panties and whipped them to the floor.

"Step out of them," he demanded.

She obeyed, surrounded by the four of us. She was gloriously nude while the rest of us remained dressed. Her breathing was ragged, and she clenched her fingers tightly.

The tension was delicious.

"Kiss me, baby," Rand said.

She positioned herself next to him on the sofa.

"No, stay right here. Bend down to kiss me," he said in a quiet voice. "But open your legs a little first."

She looked at him with a fierce gaze and moved her feet

several inches apart. She placed her hands on the sofa back on either side of his head and bent at a ninety-degree angle. The result was a beautiful one, with her ass up in the air for the remaining three of us to appreciate.

Hot damn.

29

KEALY

HOLY MOTHER OF GOD, I WAS BENT OVER FOR ALL THE
world to see. And you know what? I loved it.

Naughty me. Who knew?

While I was leaning into Rand, kissing and nibbling his
lips, there were three gorgeous male models—*my* gorgeous
male models—behind me getting ready have their way
with me. I was so excited that my legs trembled, threat-
ening to drop me to my knees. Which wouldn't have been
so bad, really.

Someone's hands—I had no idea whose—smoothed
over my ass so lightly, I broke out in goosebumps. They
were quickly followed by a tongue that ran the length of
my slit, first teasing my clit, ready to explode from the
sensation, and then to my opening. I felt moisture on the
inside of my legs.

I couldn't hide how turned on I was. And I didn't really want to, anyway.

After teasing my opening, the tongue wandered past my pussy to the sensitive spot between it and my ass. Christ, I nearly went through the roof when I felt that and just when I thought that by itself might make me explode in orgasm, the tongue was on my asshole.

Oh. My. God.

I couldn't help it. I pushed my ass right back into whoever's face was behind me. There was no way to stop it.

As I did, two fingers plunged in my pussy and started to pump, first stretching me open, and when they were nice and soaked, fucking me as deeply as they could. I moaned into Rand's mouth and buried my head in his shoulder, too distracted to keep kissing.

While my ass was being licked and my pussy pumped, Marlon put one foot up on the sofa cushion beside me. He made quick work of his belt and fly and presented me with his beautiful brown cock. As he pressed it to my lips, I took the opportunity to savor the glistening drop of precum that seeped out when he squeezed his cockhead for me. Before I licked it off, I gazed up at him and found him looking down at me with a blissful smile.

"Take it, baby," he said. "Eat my cock."

I needed no further encouragement, especially since Rand in front of me was pulling and twisting my nipples, and someone else was pressuring my asshole with what felt like two digits. The fourth guy—either Cross or Shane—had reached under me to play with my clit.

If I died right then and there, I would have died happy. No, happier than happy.

But I didn't die.

"God, baby."

It was Shane's Irish voice.

"Your pussy is so tight."

All I could do was moan with a mouthful of Marlon's cock banging against the back of my throat.

"You gonna come for us, baby?" Rand asked as he twisted my nipples to the point where I had tears in my eyes.

The hand working my clit made faster circles, and I pistoned Marlon's cock from the head down to his balls and back as all four guys worked me with an urgent, primal hunger.

Blood roared through my ears, and my vision blurred. Marlon started to spurt in my mouth, and I swallowed as fast as I could. The feel of him coming released my own orgasm, which rushed over me in violent shudders. Several hands caught me as my knees buckled and held me until the waves ceased their crashing. Rand, still seated, pulled me into his arms where he cradled me and stroked my hair.

"Oh, my god. You guys. Too much. So amazing..." I mumbled.

"Shhh, baby," Rand whispered, kissing me on the

temple. He reached for a throw on the back of the sofa and gathered it around me.

"You good, darlin'?" Shane asked.

I shook some of the cobwebs out. I wanted to be alert for what came next.

"Yes, yes I am. That was amazing." I slid off Rand's lap and pulled the throw tightly around myself. The room was suddenly chilled.

Or was that just me? Cross and Rand both had little beads of sweat across their foreheads, and Marlon and Shane had gone to the kitchen to get us all big tumblers of water.

"Wow," I said, shaking my head as I looked from one of my gorgeous guys to the other.

When I'd stopped shivering, I stood and walked around the room, picking up my scattered clothing.

"What's the rush, darlin'? You got somewhere to go?" Marlon asked.

Out of all the guys, he was the most intuitive. And his instincts were usually right on.

I jumped into my underwear and pulled on my shirt and jeans. I knew the guys would be wondering what the hell I was up to, but our lovely, amazing, earth-shattering session had just cemented something for me. Something I had to share.

"Guys. I've made a decision." I looked at all their beautiful faces.

"I can't choose just one of you. I'm not going to. Hurting any of you would break me like I've never been broken before." I shook my head hard, sucking in a small sob I'd hoped I could hide.

"Kealy, c'mon," Cross said. I pictured him with his little Joey, and my heart split down the middle.

"Because I can't choose any one of you, I am not choosing at all. I'm going to leave town, go to California or someplace sunny, and start over. New York isn't working for me." I stood, frantically searching for my purse. I needed my phone to call Marina.

Shane stood, too, and reached for my arm. But he wasn't fast enough. I avoided his touch by spinning on my heel and running for the door. Before any of them knew what was happening, I was running down the hall toward an open elevator door. When it opened to the lobby, I ran like hell and grabbed a cab that had just started to pull away from the curb.

It was like it was meant to happen, my getting the hell out of there.

"Here, sweetie," Marina said, handing me some milky chai tea. I'd never even heard of chai before I'd met her. Actually, I hadn't heard of a lot of things she taken the time to introduce me to.

"So, were they pressuring you or something? I mean, what happened? It seemed like things were perking along so well."

I dabbed my eyes and blew my nose. Poor Marina had

dealt with a lot of my tears, lately. But there was no other shoulder I'd rather cry on.

"I like them all, Marina. I thought I'd be able to choose just one. How stupid of me. They're all amazing, and they care about me. *Me.*"

Did I still not believe I deserved to be cared about? Some wounds just never healed, did they?

She leaned forward in her chair. "Of course, they care about you. Why would that surprise you? You're smart, beautiful, kind, and a kick-ass designer to boot."

I looked down at my hands, embarrassed as hell. Marina was my biggest fan—had been since I first met her. Her support never wavered.

"Marlon offered to finance me," I said in a quiet voice.

"He *what?*"

I nodded. "He wants to finance my collection." My eyes flooded with tears again, and my face crumbled. "But I can't accept it. It wouldn't be right."

"So, you gave up four great guys *and* an offer to help get your business started?" She shook her head.

Yeah. It had been that kind of night.

MARINA WALKED me to the guest room that was my home away from home—but which I guessed would be my full-on home for the near future. The sewing machine from Forest had been delivered, and she'd had it set up in the corner. She'd even gone to my apartment and gathered the rest of my fabric, sketchbooks, patterns—everything I needed to dive into making my sample set. She gave me a kiss goodnight on my temple.

Before I dozed off, I reached for my cellphone. "Fantine?" I said, when her sleepy voice answered.

"Oh, hi, Keal. Are you at one of the guys' places?" she asked.

"No. I'm at Marina's in New Jersey." I heard rustling as she propped herself up in bed.

"Why? Why aren't you with the guys?" She made it all sound so normal.

"I broke it off with them," I said, fresh tears rolling down my cheeks. God, I was getting tired of this crying shit.

"*What?*" she said in a drawn-out whisper. "You did? Why?"

"I couldn't do it. I couldn't choose just one."

"Aw, c'mon. There wasn't one of them better than the others? Didn't at least a couple of them bug the shit out of you? Like chew with his mouth open? Use the wrong fork? Tip like a cheapskate?"

"If only it were that easy. The problem was, I love them all."

Oh, shit. I'd just said the *L* word.

"Wow. Just wow. So, be with all of them," she said.

I settled into the bed Marina had made up for me. The one I used to make when I worked for her.

"I don't see how I could." God, the bed felt good. I

hadn't realized how freaking exhausted I was until I crawled under its fluffy down comforter.

"Look, Kealy," Fantine said.

I recognized that stern voice.

"Don't throw the baby out with the bath water. You know how many people would like for one person to love them. And you have four!"

But I didn't have four. I had none.

Or did I?

30

SHANE

AH, THE LOVELY KEALY. POOR THING HIGHTAILED IT OUT OF Rand's like her ass was on fire or something.

I'd wanted to chase after her. So had Marlon and Rand. But Cross—maybe because he was a father, I don't really know—insisted we let her go. She had to 'do her thing', as he put it.

Americans have the strangest sayings.

I didn't know what would happen with our girl. I mean, she said she wanted out.

But was that what she *really* wanted? It was hard for me to fathom running away from love. It seemed there was so little of it in the world that when it came your way, you needed to cherish it like a baby.

But, each to his—or her—own. I'd gotten some news

earlier that day that had nearly pushed thoughts of Kealy from my mind.

Nearly, but not completely.

I'd finished a photo shoot just in time to head down to the community center for the day's basketball practice. There were times I didn't feel like making the trek, but the minute I saw those kids' faces, my energy came rushing back, and the hour we had together flew by.

"Mr. Mooney!" one of the more enthusiastic kids yelled as I entered the gym. The kids loved the center so much, and our team, that they often came early and just hung out while they waited for practice time. "Mrs. Hill needs to see you in the office," he added.

"Okay, guys," I said to a chorus of *oooh, Mr. Mooney's in trouble*, "start with your warm up drill. I'll be right back." I jogged across the gym floor to the office of the director, a motherly woman I'd come to adore.

"Shane," she said, pointing to a chair, "how are you, honey?"

"I'm well, I am. And how's my favorite girl?" I asked.

She threw her head back and laughed loudly enough to shake the room. I loved that about her.

"I'm better now that you're here," she laughed.

"The kids told me you wanted to see me?"

Her smiling face turned serious, and she nodded, flipping through some papers on her desk. She pulled a business card from under the mess on her desk and thrust it at me.

New York Police Department

"What do they want?" I asked, turning it over in my fingers.

She folded her hands onto her desk. "Honey, it looks like they caught the guys who attacked you."

For a moment, the room spun, and I grabbed onto the arms of the chair I'd sat in. *Hold on, buddy.* My mouth went dry, as the day of the mugging came rushing back to me like it had just happened.

"Really?" I said, swallowing hard.

"Call this detective. Looks like they are bringing your guys to justice." She looked at me, and for a moment, I could see the tired in her eyes. It reminded me of the tired in my mother's eyes—the look of a woman who does for everyone else before she thinks of herself.

I looked the card over and stuck it in my back pocket.

"I'll call him after practice. The kids are waiting," I said.

"Okay, baby. I hope this isn't throwing you off. It's a good thing, you know. They won't be able to do this to anybody else."

I had to admit, I went through basketball practice with the kids like a robot on autopilot. Mrs. Hill's words *had* thrown me off, not that it was her intention. They would have thrown anyone off. As much as I loved the kids, waiting one more hour before I could get in touch with the detectives was like torture.

When they were finally gone, and I'd spent as little time

chatting with the parents as was possible without being rude —especially toward some of the moms who liked to make it abundantly clear that they were single and available. I climbed to the highest row in the bleachers and dialed the detective who'd been working on my case since the attack happened.

He answered after one ring.

"Hi, it's Shane Mooney. You came by the community center earlier today?"

"Right, Mr. Mooney. Thank you for getting back to me so fast. I have some good news for ya. Turns out we got all the guys who attacked you. Your beating was caught on video camera as you know, and it just took us a bit of time to get someone in the neighborhood to tell us where the find the young men. They're all in custody now."

Holy shit.

"Geez. I don't know what to say. I thought news like this would feel like a relief but I am just kind of numb," I said.

"That's to be expected, Mr. Mooney. You went through a terrible thing."

I took a deep breath. "What are the next steps?"

"You need to come in and ID the guys."

"Okay," I said. I was short on words, unusual for me.

"Mr. Mooney, this is very positive. Those were bad young men, and hopefully they'll be put away for a long time. They don't deserve to be on the street."

"Right. Thank you, Officer."

I'd been waiting for that moment for so long that it was almost a let down. Actually, it *was* a let down. I'd expected to feel a certain level of satisfaction, on a revenge sort of scale. But instead, I just felt sad. The kids who'd attacked me, well, their lives were essentially over.

But one positive thing I could do was make sure none of the kids on my basketball team ever turned to that type of crime.

That's why I was doing the coaching—and I hadn't even realized it. Basketball, and those beautiful ten-year-olds' faces, were healing me.

I wasn't doing shit for them. They were doing it all for me.

I WALKED to the subway in a daze, my usual vigilance about the neighborhood forgotten, when my phone buzzed.

It was a text from Cross.

can you come over? kealy wants to talk to us.

sure. when?

now.

okay. on my way.

It was a day full of goddamn surprises.

31

KEALY

FANTINE'S WORDS KEPT ME UP ALL NIGHT IN MY LITTLE BED in Marina's guest room. I was beyond exhausted, and yet my brain had no intention of slowing down. But the torture of insomnia had clarified my thoughts. I knew what I wanted. I knew what I needed. And I had something to get off my chest. So I called a meeting.

I started with Cross. He was usually the easiest to reach, probably having something to do with being a dad.

"Cross?" My heart was pounding.

"Hey. Is that you, Kealy?" he asked.

I took a deep breath. "Yeah, it is. How are ya?"

"I should be asking you how you are," he said.

"I know. I wanted to talk to you and the other guys. Do you think you could pull everyone together?" I asked, picking a spot of lint off my skirt.

"Sure. When?" Joey jabbered in the background. I pictured his fat arms and legs and how he laughed when I kissed them.

"Well, do you think we could do tonight?"

"I don't know. Let me text everyone to see if they're free."

"I really appreciate it. Thanks, Cross."

NOT FIFTEEN MINUTES later I got a text from Cross that our gathering was on. Now all I had to do was screw up about as much courage as I'd ever been able to. More than when I walked through the doors for the first time at Marina's grand home. More than my first day in college. And more than I'd needed each time I entered a new foster home.

But I could do it, because I'd done it before.

When I arrived at Cross's place, the guys were already there. They greeted me one-by-one, with hugs and kisses that were warm but not overtly sexual. They were giving me space.

Another thing I loved about them.

As soon as I sat down, Rand stood.

"Kealy, thanks for bringing us together. We guys talked and have a few things to say, which we hope you'll listen to."

"Well...I was kind of hoping I could say a few things, get them off my chest..." I stammered. Wasn't *I* the one who'd called the meeting?

He continued in spite of my protest. "Kealy, we don't want you to feel you have to choose one of us. We *all* want to be with you. We want to share, as you know," he said.

"But—" I started.

Marlon popped to his feet. "Rand is right, baby. You don't need to pressure yourself to choose. That's just not necessary. We all want to be with you."

"Well, I—" I said, to no avail. Seemed it was Shane's turn.

"Love," he said, gesturing widely, "don't be hasty. Don't make any decisions you'll regret."

They all looked at each other, heads nodding. They were all on the same page. Now I had to get them on mine.

"Okay," I said.

Brows furrowed and confusion crossed the faces I looked at.

"Yes," I said.

Rand shook his head. "Kealy, I'm not sure you're listening—"

"But I am listening. You are the ones who aren't."

They finally shut up and just stared at me.

"I'm saying yes. I want to be with all of you. I will be with all of you."

Smiles broke across all their faces. Marlon and Shane high-fived each other as Cross ran to me. With his arms around my waist, he lifted me and twirled me around the room.

"Okay, okay, you can put me down now," I said.

"No, I don't think I can," he said.

WHEN I GOT to the office the next day, the room where all the junior designers worked was eerily quiet. In fact, I could have sworn I heard a couple people sniffling and blowing their noses.

I guessed I'd missed some sort of drama. Since I'd started staying at Marina's place in New Jersey, I usually ended up being the last person in the office in the morning. Not wanting to draw attention, I woke up my computer, settled in, and didn't say a word to anyone.

"Kealy, can I see you in my office, please?" Forest's voice boomed.

Shit.

Did he find out about that fabric I helped myself to? But it was scrap, and he'd always told me to take what I wanted.

Or was he going to take back the sewing machine over some perceived slight? Nah, he wasn't petty like that.

Maybe it was related to my insistence that Muse had pirated my work…and my unwillingness to let it go? Shit, I should have just kept my mouth shut and my head down.

"C'mon in, Kealy. Grab a seat right there," he said, pointing. "I need to talk to you about Muse," he said.

My stomach dropped. Oh, my god, in addition to stealing my work, had he also said terrible things about me?

Forest lowered his voice since his loft office didn't

afford a lot of privacy. "You may have noticed that Muse is not here this morning."

"Oh, no, I hadn't noticed—I mean, yes. Yes, I noticed," I lied.

Way to draw attention to your lateness, dumbass.

He looked confused at my indecision. "Okay. Well. I wanted to let you know Muse doesn't work here any more."

Huh?

"Muse? He left?" I said. It came out as more of a squeak.

He looked down at his hands. He always picked his cuticles when he was under stress. As a result, they perpetually looked like raw hamburger meat. It was the only thing about him that wasn't perfect.

"He didn't leave. He was escorted out. Fired."

Fired? No, I was sure I didn't hear that right. "Sorry? What did you say, Forest?" I asked.

He nodded slightly. "Muse is gone. Asked to leave the company. Fired."

Oh. My. God.

"Wh…why?" I gripped the sides of my chair.

He leaned back in his chair and stretched, hands behind his head. Something about him looked tired. Weary, even.

He shook his head slowly. "He'd been working with one of our suppliers overseas. He sent them an order and when the goods never arrived here, the bookkeeper looked into it. Turned out, Muse had been placing orders with a fake company and siphoning our payments to his own account."

I was speechless. Couldn't think of a single thing to say. I knew Muse had stolen my work, but stolen *money from the company?*

And Forest could tell.

"Yeah, I was pretty shocked, myself." He looked out his office window for a moment and then back to me. "We went through his desk and computer and not only found he'd stolen your designs, but also emailed a friend to brag about it."

My hand flew to my mouth, and a tear slid down my face. But it wasn't about being vindicated by the exposure of Muse's wrongdoings. Forest had been deeply deceived, and I knew what that was like.

"I owe you an apology," he said.

He did owe me an apology. I nodded in acceptance. But I didn't blame him. Muse was cute and charming. He'd fooled me and Forest, and others, I'm sure.

"I'm sorry this happened to you, Forest," I said quietly.

"Me too. Me too, Kealy." He rose to his feet. "I'll find some way to make it up to you. I'm sorry I doubted your story. It was wrong, and I regret it. You're a great designer, and I should have known your work when I saw it."

I looked down at my hands, embarrassed by his shame. "Forest, you've done so much for me..." But I stopped. The lump in my throat made it too hard to say any more.

"Okay. Thanks, kiddo."

I followed him to his door, and before I left, he turned back to me. "If there is anything you ever need, anything I can ever do for you, all you have to do is ask."

It was a sincere offer, and I knew he meant every word of it.

"Well, there is something I'd like to talk to you about…" I said.

32

CROSS

I BENT TO STRAIGHTEN JOEY'S TIE AND SMOOTH BACK HIS blond hair. The hairdressers had put gel in it, to my dismay. But I had to admit, it was pretty freaking cute. I took him by the hand and led him, in line with the other models, to the backstage curtain where we were to wait for our cue. I crouched down to his level.

"Okay, little man. What are we gonna do here?"

"Hold Daddy's hand," he said, holding out his arm to prove he knew what he was doing.

"Good boy. And you will not let go, right?" I asked.

"Nope, no, no. Daddy's hand."

He shook his head, knocking a few gelled strands of hair out of place. I hoped the hairdresser wouldn't notice—he looked even better a little mussed.

The audience went silent, and the stage lights dimmed.

The music cued, and Kealy ran over to me, clipboard in hand.

"Are my guys ready?" she asked, flashing Joey and me her brilliant smile.

I looked down at my guy, who just gazed back up at our girl. He adored her just like the rest of us did.

"Okay." She gave me a quick peck on the cheek and went down the line checking in with the other models.

The stage manager pulled back the curtain and waved at my Joey and me. My boy and I walked hand in hand to the opening, and when the lights came up on the runway, we started to walk.

I'd never done a show before with a kid, much less my son, so it was a good thing we practiced. The little dude could only walk so fast, but his smile was bright and his poise impeccable. When the audience began its *oohs* and *aahs* at seeing him dressed just like me, only in smaller clothes, he started to wave back at them like he was in a freaking parade.

I guess to him, that's what it was.

When we got to the end of the catwalk, the camera flashes were like nothing I'd ever seen before. I was a seasoned model, used to being photographed. But I'd never seen the fashion press go crazy like this before. Nervous about how Joey would react, I bent to pick

him up, smiling the whole way, and carried him on my hip, with one arm, the rest of the way back up the catwalk. I stopped in the middle as we always did to turn to give the audience one more look, when I decided to ham it up a bit.

I gave Joey a quick kiss on the cheek, and he nestled his head onto my shoulder.

It was fucking perfect, and the crowd went wild.

It had been Forest's idea to do a daddy-and-me collection of mini duds for Kealy's debut show. Who knew if there was a market for them, but we sure as hell were the darlings, if only for a moment, of the fashion industry.

Forest had been one of Kealy's biggest supporters when she told him she wanted to go out on her own. I had to hand it to him. A lot of other bosses would have been dicks about something like that.

"Oh, my god, it was just perfect!" Kealy said, jumping up and down like a kid. "Did you like it, Joey?" she asked, crouching to his level.

"Joey is model," he said shyly, ducking behind my legs.

"Guess it runs in the family," Kealy said to me.

One of her staff tapped her on the arm. "Kealy, we have a broken zipper over here. We need you."

She gave me another kiss on the cheek and sprinted off, probably to try and fix something Rand had made a mess of. He was always busting buttons and zippers at these shows. I loved the guy but he had all the finesse of a rhino. Off the runway, that was.

Shane and Marlon returned from their strut on the catwalk and rushed to their changing stations for their next get-up. I had no changes in this show, I guess because they wanted to keep Joey and me in matching outfits. It was fun to watch the backstage hustle and bustle for a change, rather than being in the middle of it. I brought

Joey over to the snack table, which was always a waste because models barely ate, and let him chow on a donut. He normally wasn't allowed sweets, but I knew it would keep him happy and quiet, at least for the fifteen minutes or so left in the show.

Marlon waved me over after he exited the stage. He was done with his outfit changes, so just had to wait until the last walk when we all went down together, before he got back in his street clothes.

"Dude, you and the little man rocked it," he said, wiping some sugar off the corner of Joey's mouth with his thumb.

"Uncle Mar," Joey said. "Donut." He patted his potbelly, and Marlon gave him a kiss on the cheek.

Joey might be without his mother, but there would be no lack of love in his life.

"Never thought I'd hit the runway with my kid, but I loved every second of it. I can't wait to do it again." I took in the controlled chaos surrounding us. "It's amazing, Marlon. I mean, look at all this," I said, gesturing at the room.

Racks full of Kealy's new designs, the fashion press, makeup artists and models, photographers—she'd not only pulled it all off, but she had done so to major accolades from industry movers and shakers.

A thunderous applause erupted from the audience, signaling the end of the show. We hustled up to the curtain where Kealy and the other guys waited for us. She extended her hands to Cross and Marlon. I positioned Joey between Shane and myself, and we each took one of his hands.

The stage manager pulled back the curtain to let us on the runway, and we joined Kealy as she bowed, waved, and threw kisses to an audience giving her a standing ovation.

It was the first time she'd appeared in public with the four of us guys since she'd agreed to let us share her.

And it wouldn't be the last.

CHAPTER 33

KEALY

I WAS BEYOND EXHAUSTED, HAVING WORKED AROUND THE clock for weeks getting my collection ready for the Fashion Week shows.

Was it worth it?

I'd just delivered my own designs to the definitive approval of the fashion world, and I was bowing on the runway with my four loves. Well, five, if you counted little Joey.

So, yeah, it was worth it. Fuck, yeah, in fact.

It's funny how life gave you second chances sometimes. And third, and fourth ones. Maybe even fifths if you were super lucky.

Even Muse, the thief, was getting a second chance. Forest had agreed not to press charges against him. But he told him not to work in fashion again. Last I heard, he'd left town. Moved to Miami or someplace like that to work in a sandwich shop.

As camera flashes blinded us and applause shook the room, I took a couple bows. I felt utterly ridiculous, but it was an end-of-show tradition among designers.

Speaking of designers, I peered into the front row on my right and looked down on Forest, who was on his feet and clapping harder than anyone in the room. If I wasn't mistaken, he had tears in his eyes. I released Cross and Marlon's hands and gestured toward my mentor and biggest fan. The applause got even louder, if that were possible. Everyone knew I owed endless thanks to Forest. I'd be nothing without his support.

Actually, I was lucky enough to have the support of several amazing people, not least of which were my guys.

In the few months since I'd gone out on my own, a lot had changed.

Rand, my muscular, earring-wearing love, was finishing up his finance degree while working as my company's CFO. Thanks to his connections in the business, he was doing a bang-up job of wrangling investors who believed in my work. It was a stamp of approval that I couldn't have hoped for. And yet, it came my way.

He was eager to give up modeling, but he had promised to keep doing my shows. He couldn't get off that easy. He was probably the only finance guy in New York with a modeling side hustle. The other guys thought it was funny as hell.

My beautiful brown-skinned Marlon was the company's president. As the majority investor, he'd built a small board of directors to guide us. And guess what? His dad joined. Yup, after years of resisting each other, Marlon and his father had found common ground.

And their matching bald heads were freaking adorable.

The dreamy Shane, my red-headed Irishman, had seen his attackers put behind bars. He'd stopped absentmind-edly rubbing the raised scar on his chest. It was almost as if it had gone away altogether. And like Marlon and Rand, he was phasing out his modeling gigs. He'd saved enough money that he was now expanding the operations of the community center and building kids' sports teams as fast as he could find volunteers to coach them. My heart was so full of pride, and even more so when he'd asked me to design team shirts for the center. I was honored to be able to contribute in my own small way.

And Cross, father of Joey, his mini-me, was the only one of the group who planned to continue modeling. It gave him the flexibility he needed to be a single parent and provided a nice living at the same time. Of course, he'd be in all my shows and advertisements, as would Shane, if I could manage to tear him away from the basketball court.

It was incredible how the gods of good fortune had smiled down on me. There I stood on the runway of my first fashion show, with my loves at my side. I knew things wouldn't always be smooth sailing, but with the support of these amazing, gorgeous men, any bumps that lay in the road ahead would be barely noticeable. One day, maybe they'd cease to exist. Until then, we had each other.

And that was more than enough.

I hope you loved reading this book as much as I loved writing it.
Find all Mika Lane books here:
https://mikalaneshop.com/

ABOUT THE AUTHOR

Dear Reader:

I'm USA TODAY bestselling romance author Mika Lane, and am OBSESSED with bringing you sassy, steamy stories with imperfect heroines and the bad-a*s dudes they bring to their knees. I'll always bring you my signature humor and heat, topped off with a modern-day happily ever after.

My first book ever was *The Day I Ate the Milkyway,* a true fourth-grade masterpiece illustrated with crayons and bound with construction paper and glue. Nowadays, steamy romance gives purpose to my days and nights as I create worlds and characters that tickle the imagination. I live in magical Northern California with my own handsome alpha dude, sometimes known as Mr. Mika Lane, and two devilish cats named Chuck and Murray.

A dual citizen of the United States and Ireland, I have on more than one occasion spent my last dollar on a plane ticket somewhere, and am always planning my next escape. I often try new recipes on unsuspecting friends, search out hiding places to read undisturbed, and sadly kill every houseplant I bring home.

I LOVE to hear from readers when I'm not dreaming up naughty tales to share. Visit my online shop https://mikalaneshop.com/ and say hello https://mikalaneshop.com/pages/meet-mika.

xoxo, Mika